The Story:

of Love, Loss, and Memories

By Lynda Lahman

Cover photography by Peter Vordenberg

ISBN-10: 1545287716

ISBN-13: 978-1545287712

For Ray and Amy who showed me what true love could be and to Terry for helping me experience it for myself.

All of these lines across my face

Tell you the story of who I am

So many stories of where I've been

And how I got to where I am

But these stories don't mean anything

When you've got no one to tell them to

It's true, I was made for you.

Brandi Carlisle, *The Story*

Helen

Prologue

I caught part of my mother's conversation as I walked down the hallway toward the living room. Hesitating at the door, I listened, intrigued, as she shared an old childhood story with one of her friends.

"I went into the garage for just a minute to check on the wash. The kids were both in their rooms asleep. As I came back in, I heard the beginnings of the baby fussing and starting to wake up. I tiptoed past her door, hoping to get the load of towels I'd taken out of the dryer folded before she really began to cry, but as I passed Gary's room I noticed his bed was empty."

There was a catch in Ann's voice as she paused, recalling the events of that faraway day.

"The baby's sounds became more insistent, finally bursting into her typical wake-up cries. I went in and picked her up, then called for Gary, but there was no answer. Where could he have gone?"

Leaning against the wall, I sensed the fear still present in my mother's voice despite the passage of more than fifty years. "He wasn't in the living room or the kitchen. I searched the house, every nook and cranny, every closet and cupboard, yelling his name. And then I saw the front door, barely ajar. *Oh my God, I thought. How could he have reached the handle? How could he have opened it by himself? Had I somehow forgotten to close it securely?* Now I was in a full panic but trying to stay calm for the baby's sake. How long had he been gone? Running down the front stairs I raced around the yard, praying I'd find him playing in the sandbox, but he was nowhere to be found.

"As I passed the kitchen window I heard the phone ringing. Still holding Shelly I ran up the steps, ripped open the side door and grabbed the receiver before the caller could hang up."

"'Hello! Hello!' Breathing hard, I nearly shouted into the phone, hoping against hope it was one of the neighbors calling to tell me Gary had wandered to their house to play. Instead I heard a deep, unfamiliar voice and my heart stopped." She paused, and then I heard her voice again, repeating what she had been told over the phone.

"'Mrs. Wylings, I believe we have your son here. It seems he walked down to the playground all by himself. One of the other mothers recognized him,' the policeman's voice was calm on the other end of the line. 'Would you like to come get him? Or should one of our patrolmen bring him up to your place?'"

The tension in my mother's voice evaporated. "I'd almost had a heart attack. That kid! How he had managed to open the front door, get down the steps and cross Atlantic Avenue, a major street with lots of traffic, all by himself I'll never know."

She could now laugh at the memory, knowing Gary had been found safe and was sitting across from her in his living room, indulging our mother's need to tell this story to anyone who would listen. I knew he'd have preferred she not bring up tales of growing up, but once she got going on something we both knew better than to try and stop her. She'd only make a scene, and no one needed that tonight.

"He loved the playground, always begging me to take him there so he could climb up the slide and wait for me to catch him as he came down, but I never once imagined he'd go there alone. He was only two-and-a-half-years-old! To this day I have no idea how he even knew how to get there. He must have paid far more attention when we were out walking than I knew!"

Lost in the story and my own memories, my mother's laughter snapped me back into the present. I turned around and walked to the kitchen, joining my husband who was just finishing making a pot of coffee. I opened the cabinet above the counter to grab us each a cup and suddenly paused mid-reach.

"Are you okay?' Alan looked at me quizzically. 'Need me to help with something?"

The events of that day had been etched in my mind for so long; for years I'd remembered it clearly, despite my young age. But *I* was the one who had climbed up the slide, crossing the busy intersection and alarming my mother with my apparent lack of fear. *I* had been startled when the woman sharply called my name, wondering why I was there without my parents. *I* was the one the policeman took gently by the hand and led to the station next to the park.

I sat quietly on the chair while I watched him run his fingers down the page of the thick white book until he found the name he was looking for and dialed the number, calling my mother on the big black phone. I knew it was *me* who had seen my mother, tears of relief streaming down her face, crying out my name as she ran through the door and scooped me up in her arms.

Except as I listened to Ann tell the tale tonight, for the first time it dawned on me that it couldn't possibly have been me who crossed the busy street to play at the park. I'd been the one in the crib; I'd only been six-months-old when it happened. How had I gotten the story so wrong for all these years?

And maybe, more importantly, how do we ever know which of our memories—our stories—are the real ones?

Chapter 1

Finishing up case notes from the last client of the day, I checked my office voicemail one final time before shoving the file into the drawer and locking my desk. No messages; a good sign. No last minute emergencies, no calls to return that might keep me late. I glanced out the window. Barely five-thirty and it was starting to darken outside. I'd noticed the increasing crispness in the air, though it was still more than a month before the clocks turned back. Fall was coming too quickly; with its shorter days I'd soon be driving to and from work without seeing light at all. A full schedule of appointments tomorrow and then on to Phoenix for an eagerly anticipated four days filled with professional workshops, catching up with colleagues, and sunshine. It'd been a long stretch without a break. I couldn't wait.

I grabbed my rain jacket off the rack in the corner of the room and slung it over my shoulder. The morning had started with the typical Seattle drizzle, but the promised sun break had finally appeared; no sense putting it on just to drive home. I picked my purse up off the floor under my desk and searched for my cell phone tucked inside. Turning off airplane mode, I clicked off the table lamps, took one last glance around, and started down the hallway I shared with five other therapists. Only Lisa, in the office next to mine, was left, slaving away at her computer, most likely working on one of the reports her work with children of divorcing couples often required.

"See you Monday," I said, poking my head in to let her know I was taking off.

"Yup, see you Monday," she replied as she stopped to stretch back in her chair. "Have fun; sure wish I were going with you. A few days of warmth and light would be very welcome after all the rain we've had the last few weeks!"

"Thanks, I intend to." I paused for a second in the doorway, glad someone else was still working and I didn't have to close up the whole suite. "Should be some good stuff. I'll impress you all with my brilliance when I get back." I liked our group discussions each week when we met for consultation. It kept me up to date about current therapy approaches and gave me a place to get help whenever I felt stymied with a client's issues. The confidentiality and support of co-workers was one of the benefits of working in an office rather than off somewhere, isolated by myself.

As I started back down the hall I felt my phone vibrate, startling me. Looking down, I was surprised to see I'd missed three calls, all from numbers I didn't recognize. Hardly anyone knew this number, and clients left messages on my office voicemail. Alan even used that line while I was at work, knowing I'd be far more likely to return his call since I always turned off my cell when in session.

"Mind if I get this? I've already shut down my office," I inquired, sticking my head back through Lisa's open door. She waved me in. Tossing my purse and coat on an empty chair, I sat on her couch, curious who would be calling. Tapping the button for voicemail, I entered my four-digit code and obediently hit '3' when prompted.

"Hi, you don't know me, but my name's Molly and I live across the street from Helen and Bruce. They're delightful neighbors. Helen

14

often comes over to play with my twins and they absolutely adore her," a strange voice spoke rapidly, an urgency underlying the benign words. "But in the last few weeks I've noticed she hasn't looked very well; I don't think they're eating much. I hope you don't think I'm being presumptuous, but I wonder if they might benefit from Meals On Wheels or some other program. I've done some research and I have some phone numbers if you'd like them." The woman left her phone number and hung up.

That's odd. I looked over at Lisa, confused. "This is really weird. Some woman I've never met is calling me about my step-grandmother, says she's not eating." I clicked on the next message as Lisa paused her typing, turning to face me.

"Shelly, this is Myron, Bruce's son. We've never spoken, but I found your number in Helen's phone book. It took a lot of digging to figure out her filing system. Anyway, the reason I am calling is to inform you that I'm coming on Friday to move my dad to a nursing home. His health's deteriorating and I'm concerned. Wanted to let you know." The stiffness in his voice was even more disturbing than his words. What kind of person would be so cruel as to leave such an abrupt message, having never met or spoken with me?

"What the hell?" The intensity in my tone startled Lisa.

"You okay?" she whispered, as if the voicemail caller could overhear. "What's wrong?"

"I've got no idea. It's all got to do with my grandmother; none of it's making any sense." I struggled to process what I had just heard. "I really don't know. Hang on a sec."

I hesitated, my mind swirling. *What was going on with Helen?* I clicked on the third message.

"Shelly, it's Molly again, the neighbor across the street from your grandmother. I saw Myron after I left the first message. He takes Bruce and Helen to the store every Wednesday and I caught him today as he was leaving, hoping to ask about the Meals on Wheels. He said he's moving Bruce Friday. I'm really worried about Helen. I don't know what'll she'll do without him." There was an edge to her voice that hadn't been in the first voicemail. Once again she left her phone number.

"It's some kind of crisis with my grandmother. I gotta deal with this, figure out what's happening." I stood abruptly, scooped up my things and went back to my office, switching on the ceiling light. Pulling out my chair I sat down, dreading what else I might find out. I took a deep breath and dialed.

"Hi, Molly, this is Shelly Johnson, Helen's granddaughter. I just got your messages. Can you help me out a bit? This is all news to me. I talk to Helen every few weeks or so, and had no idea things were this bad." I tried to keep my voice calm and reasonable, concealing the tension building inside.

"I'm glad you called. I hope I'm not overstepping my place, but I'm really worried about Helen. She stops by here every few days to say hi to the twins. The kids love her, see her as a kind of surrogate grandmother." The words poured out, almost apologetically. "I didn't know what else to do. When we moved in two years ago we exchanged emergency contact information, you know, in case we ever needed it. I never thought I would, but I'm happy now we did." I listened patiently, waiting for her to continue.

"Anyway, I thought you should know what was happening. I was thinking Meals on Wheels would help, but I guess it's worse than I imagined."

"Molly, I really appreciate your call and concern. I'm surprised is all. Myron also left a message about moving Bruce." *He doesn't seem to give a damn about Helen or the impact on her. His only worry is Bruce. There's no way Helen can handle this alone. How in the hell did this happen? What in God's name is he thinking?* I could feel my anger festering and stopped for a moment, staring at the painting above my desk to gather my thoughts before continuing. "I think it's best that I be there to see what's going on. I need to book a flight. Can I meet you when I get there?"

"Absolutely. I'll help any way I can. Like I said, I really care about Helen. Let me know what I can do," Molly replied, the relief in her voice apparent.

I hung up the phone and sat for a full minute before my brain kicked into gear, the logistics necessary to rearrange my plans taking shape. I had no time to process what was happening, I had to act. I guess thirty years as a therapist was coming in handy: don't panic; take it one step at a time.

I took a deep breath and called my husband. "Alan, I've got to go to Helen's right away," I said after giving him a brief overview of what I'd learned. "There's no one else around, and definitely no one else she trusts. It'd be good for you to come as well. It isn't going to be pretty and I'm going to need your wisdom and perspective."

"I have to be at the office tomorrow all day for a mandatory meeting, but I can leave anytime after that," he said without hesitation. His unconditional support was one of the things I loved about him. He never doubted my judgment and never questioned me when it came to family.

"I think it's easier if I stay at the office to make the arrangements; all the numbers I need are here." I had to cancel the next day's appointments, change my flight from Phoenix to San Francisco, and figure out how to get in touch with the conference folks. I doubted they'd give a refund this late, but I had no choice. "I'll call

17

you when I'm on my way home." Hanging up, I unlocked my desk drawer and began pulling out files, making careful notes as I called each client.

Lisa poked her head in. "Got my last report finished and I'm heading out, but I wanted to see if I could be of any help before I leave."

I appreciated her offer, but there really wasn't much she could do. "If you can shut down the waiting room and kitchen, and let everyone here know what's up when you get in tomorrow, that'd be a few less things for me to do. I'll email you when I have some idea of what's going on."

"Sure thing." Lisa smiled. "I hope it's not as dire as it sounds. Good luck."

I'd spoken with most of my clients and left messages for the others, booked my flight and made hotel arrangements when I finally glanced up at the clock. I was surprised to see it'd been almost two hours since Lisa had left but I'd accomplished most of the items on my list. I'd located a cheaper fare for Alan later in the evening and copied the paperwork needed to call the conference committee to see about a refund. I'd reserved a car and printed the information for the airport shuttle for Alan; he could make his own reservation in the morning. With not much else to do, I headed home to pack. I was already exhausted, and knew the worst was still to come.

"I'll call Helen after dinner. She's been talking about needing some help and maybe I can use that as an excuse to visit. I won't tell her I've already made plans," I told Alan as we sat down for a much-needed meal. I hadn't noticed my hunger in the whirlwind of activity. "At the very least I can get a sense of her state of mind."

I knew her number by heart; it hadn't changed in over forty years.

As I listened to the ringing I pictured the beige phone on the wall in the kitchen in the house my grandfather and Helen had shared before his death twelve years earlier. Even after his passing, very little had changed; a few of Bruce's sailing decorations replaced knick-knacks from earlier travels, and the desk in Papa Paul's office was taken over with Bruce's financial statements and magazines devoted to stocks and bonds. But the house my grandparents had moved to when I was barely ten was still a living memorial to their life together. The images provided a small comfort as I waited for Helen to answer the phone. Maybe things weren't as dramatic as everyone had made it sound.

After what felt like an eternity, I heard the somewhat breathless voice of my grandmother. "Hello? Hello? Who's calling?" The abruptness was startling. Helen was always so cheerful and polite whenever I called, happy to hear from me, and eager to chat. "Who is this?" she went on.

"Helen, it's Shelly. I was just calling to let you know I'm coming down your way tomorrow for a business meeting and thought I'd stay an extra couple of days for a visit. Will you be around?" I hoped she wouldn't see through my lie.

"Why in the world are you thinking of coming? What gave you the idea I wanted you to visit?" She was indignant. "I don't want you here. I'm too busy with Bruce."

I was shocked by her vehemence. We'd spoken a few times over the past several months, mostly pleasant conversations about the kids and the lovely weather in California. Yes, she'd complained about exhaustion and having to shoulder all the care of Bruce herself, and her dependence on Myron ever since she'd wrecked her car the previous year. After the accident, Helen was reluctant to get behind the wheel, and unfortunately, the house was quite a ways from town. Her complaints frequently centered on her feelings of isolation and her loathing to ask anyone for help.

Fiercely independent, her role had always been the caretaker, not the care recipient.

"We talked about it a few weeks ago. I thought I'd come help out. You've mentioned how tired you are, and how hard it is without a car. I figured I could drive you around, let you take care of business, whatever you need," I continued, hoping to soften Helen's resistance. "I'd love to see you."

"Well, I don't want you here. I have no idea what you'd do and I don't want to be taking care of guests now anyway." There was a nastiness in her voice I'd never heard before.

"I'm not a guest! I'm your granddaughter! You don't need to do anything. I'll stay in a hotel so you and Bruce don't need to worry about me. I just want to visit and see you."

Her behavior struck me as odd. Helen was usually overjoyed to have me come for a short stop. We'd spend our time going to lunch, sharing photographs of my latest adventures, and reminiscing about Papa Paul. Things really had deteriorated in the short time since we'd last spoken.

"It's too much; I don't want to be taking care of you on top of Bruce," she persisted.

"Well, okay, if you prefer I not come, I won't." I backed down, not wanting to push her further, while privately confirming that the decision to go was even more urgent than I had imagined only hours earlier.

"That was a weird conversation. I don't understand her resistance," I commented to Alan as I clicked off the phone. "It's bizarre; she isn't acting like herself at all. It's as if she doesn't want me to see her, which is so unlike her."

We'd always been close, even more so after the death of Papa Paul.

20

I'd been the one she'd turned to in her grief, coming to Seattle for her first two Christmases without him. That second year we giggled uncontrollably, sharing intimate secrets of her new relationship with Bruce as if we were college girls gossiping at a slumber party. They met through a support group for those grieving the loss of their spouses, and she admitted that she loved Bruce, 'although never like the way I loved your grandfather, this is different. He knows your grandfather was the love of my life, and it's okay.' Her guilt was greatly relieved when I offered my wholehearted support for this late-in-life gift of companionship. I pictured the quaint restaurant we'd gone to when we passed through town, Helen eager to introduce Bruce, and the look of peacefulness that spread over her face when it was clear we approved of her choice. How had things gone so wrong so quickly, and why hadn't I been able to detect the change sooner? Had there been signs I'd missed?

I brought my attention back to the tasks at hand. There was one left on the list. "This is the call I'm actually dreading," I said to Alan. "Remind me to stay calm and maybe I'll be able to figure out what's going on."

I looked at the notepad with Myron's number scrawled across it. *Here goes nothing.* I pressed the numbers on the keypad. *Odd I've never met him; weirder that he never called me if he had concerns. What must be going through his head that he would even consider taking Bruce away from Helen?* I listened to the ringing, half hoping no one would pick up. How could he have let things get this bad without thinking of contacting me?

"Hello?" The voice on the other end was strong and confident. Myron must have inherited Bruce's longevity genes. He had to be close to eighty; Bruce had celebrated his centennial birthday the previous spring. "Who's calling?"

"Hi, Myron. It's Helen's step-granddaughter, Shelly." I waited for confirmation before continuing. "I got your call, and one from

Molly, their neighbor. Can you fill me in on what's happening?"

"Sure. I've arranged to have Dad transferred to a skilled nursing home on Friday. Helen hasn't been feeding him and he's losing too much weight. He can't cook himself; he's too frail. If I don't get him out of there I'm worried he'll starve to death. I've tried talking to Helen, but she gets argumentative and defensive. While I have concerns about her, my job is to watch out for my dad." Myron didn't sound particularly sensitive to Helen's needs. "And I haven't told her we're moving him; don't want her doing anything crazy."

While I found myself sympathetic to his assessment of Helen reacting with anger and defensiveness, suddenly removing her partner of eleven years with no warning and no backup was outrageous. How dare he be so callous? "So you're going over on Friday, taking your dad away, and she's got no idea this is coming? What do you think will happen to her?"

"I've arranged for a social worker to be there to talk to her when we take him. Like I said, my job is to take care of my dad. I've tried reasoning with Helen to no avail. I'm sorry, but he's the one I have to worry about, not her."

I gripped the phone, appalled by Myron's lack of emotion and overwhelmed by what I'd just heard. Yes, Helen could be difficult at times, stubborn and opinionated, but she was also fiercely loyal, loving, and warm. She didn't deserve this.

"You must realize she's going to be totally freaked out. Seriously, if you can't even talk to her I doubt a social worker will be able to do much." It took all of my willpower to refrain from screaming at Myron. "I'm coming down tomorrow. She doesn't know I'm coming, so please don't say anything. She needs someone with her who cares about her when this happens." *And it clearly isn't you!* I had to bite my tongue to keep from snapping at him.

Chapter 2

"I still can't understand how he can do this to Helen." I was exhausted from lack of sleep and incredulous at Myron's insensitivity. All night I'd struggled to calm my mind down enough to nod off, only to reawaken several times replaying his words. "He was so officious. I can't believe he's Bruce's son, who's so quiet and gentle. It's unfathomable."

I glanced over at Alan, who was focused on the road, hoping to drop me off at the airport without being late to the office. Since he was flying down later, we decided to leave only one car at the airport rather than pay to park two. Our flight home was booked for Sunday; I was being optimistic things could be straightened out within the next few days.

"We don't know what Myron's been dealing with concerning Helen. As much as we both love her, we also know she can be incredibly pig-headed. She has a biting temper and once it gets going it's impossible to reason with her," Alan said, in an effort to reassure me that maybe Myron wasn't the monster I'd pictured from our first conversation. "Maybe he's simply overwhelmed himself. If he's been trying to help them out, Helen may not have allowed him to do much. She believes she knows best when it comes to caring for someone she loves, and you know how she can shut out everyone else."

I hated to admit it, but I had to acknowledge his point. I'd last seen it when Papa Paul was dying. During his final few days in the hospital, hooked to morphine to ease his suffering, Helen had fought with the staff to care for him by herself, not trusting them to do anything correctly. "Yeah, there's a fierceness to her love, and if you get on the wrong side of it, watch out. Thank God I've always been spared."

Hugging Alan goodbye at the curb, the magnitude of what I was about to face was sinking in and I wished he were going with me. I didn't want to let go, and we held each other for a minute before gently pulling apart.

"I'll be there tonight. We'll figure this out together and I'll be with you. I wish I could go now, but it won't be long." I knew he was right. Giving him one last kiss, I tugged my bag up onto the curb and waved as he got back into the car, pulled out into the maze of traffic in front of the terminal, and was gone. I was alone.

Helen doesn't want me to come. How am I going to simply show up and help out? What if she slams the door in my face, or worse, rages at me for interfering?

I settled into my window seat on the plane, thinking about my grandparents. There was comfort in remembering them, when Papa Paul was around and everything had been good. It helped distract me from the chaos I knew I was about to walk into.

The story of how they met was recited at practically every family gathering, and the love between them had been palpable to anyone who saw them together. 'A romance novel come to life' was a common description, and they had remained totally devoted to each other until his death forty-four years after they first laid eyes on each other.

24

When I was younger I'd imagined their relationship as being magical and unobtainable, a fairy tale come true, until I met Alan. My own parents had each been through several marriages, none of which had been terribly successful. Falling for Alan showed me deeply felt love wasn't a fluke; it'd been most of the other adults in my life who'd had it wrong.

Papa Paul met Helen when they had a chance encounter at a fundraiser for the local hospital in New Jersey where they were both living. He'd been unhappily married for eighteen years to his second wife, Dolly, a woman he'd proposed to on the rebound after my grandmother, his first wife, had abandoned him. Desiring companionship and validation, it was only after the wedding he learned she was a cold, unfeeling, bitter woman. How could he explain two failed relationships to his family and friends? He'd confided to me once that he'd seen a psychiatrist, seeking a cure for his depression, but the visit merely confirmed his worst fears: unless he wanted to face the shame of another divorce he was stuck. Instead, he buried himself in his work, spending hours behind his desk, building a worldwide clientele that had paid off handsomely in an ongoing succession of promotions. His presence at the hospital benefit was one of the direct results: he was representing the company at the premier gala of the year.

Helen had spent the past several years travelling the country, responding to the latest polio outbreaks, bringing her skills as a nurse to wherever she felt most needed. Her expertise had earned her a small but well-respected reputation, and her ability as a public speaker created a demand for her talks. Polio was a terrifying disease, and anyone who could share a front-line experience was in high demand. For her, the gala was just another stop on her current east coast tour, another effort to raise money to help fund the ongoing research for a successful vaccine since a cure wasn't proving to be possible.

When she rose to speak, Papa Paul found his attention slowly being pulled from the small talk he was engaged in with a gentleman next to him. He politely finished his thought and turned his eyes to the stage where the panel of experts was seated. A small, wiry woman, barely visible over the podium, was telling a story of a young patient she had recently treated.

He couldn't stop staring. *What the hell is going on?* he thought. He wasn't listening to a word she said and yet she held him spellbound. Her passion, her intensity, her smile were all so seductive. *She's so damned cute, and smart to boot! I have to meet this woman.*

As soon as the last speaker finished, he excused himself from the table and pushed his way up toward the dais, trying to appear nonchalant, but nudging anyone who got in his path. He briefly lost sight of her and panic rose up in his throat. *What if I missed her, if they spirited her away and I never see her again?*

He scanned the front of the room, trying to stay calm. She was still there, engaged in an animated conversation with an older woman dressed in a stylish business suit. She barely reached the lady's shoulders. Paul moved close enough to listen in to their chatter, ready to introduce himself when an opening occurred. It felt like forever, but they finally wrapped up and she turned to leave.

"Excuse me, my name is Paul Allaway, and I was very impressed by your talk and your work."

She paused to shake his hand. "Thank you, Mr. Allaway. I love what I do and it's nice to know it's appreciated. I hope our efforts will have the desired effect and encourage all of you to open your wallets and donate." She smiled up at him, and in that moment he knew his world was about to change forever.

"Do you have plans for this evening? Are you expected elsewhere?

I would love to hear more about your work if you don't have anything you need to do," he inquired.

"No, I have nothing planned," she replied, still smiling.

"Then would you like to do nothing together?" he asked, having no idea where the words came from or where they would lead.

The rest, as the cliché goes, is history. Neglecting for several weeks to mention that he was married, Helen was enraged when she found out. She felt tricked and ashamed; just the thought of seeing a married man violated her sense of propriety. She broke off their budding relationship repeatedly, only to be drawn back by the intensity of her feelings for him. Though he was twenty-three years older, she fell as deeply in love with Paul as he did with her. They struggled for well over a year; he didn't know a way out of his marriage, and Helen couldn't keep on as his mistress. Finally the miracle he'd been hoping for since he'd first married Dolly occurred: a way out. Paul and his brother each received a sizable inheritance from their mother's passing, which he immediately signed over to Dolly to satisfy her future needs that guaranteed both her respectability and his freedom. He had bought his future with Helen, and they could finally be together openly. They wed in a quiet, private ceremony, and a few years later, they both retired and moved to California.

"Please bring your seatbacks and tray tables to an upright and locked position in preparation for landing." The flight attendant's voice brought me sharply back to the present and to the realities I was about to face. Papa Paul has been dead twelve years. It was all on my shoulders.

Chapter 3

After checking into the hotel where Alan and I always stayed when we visited, I pushed the button on the elevator and scanned my surroundings as I waited. The building had not aged gracefully. Worn carpets and stains dotted the hallway despite the fading bird of paradise pattern designed to disguise such misuse. I stepped into the open door of the glass lift and looked out over the atrium, an indoor garden style popular at the time it was first built, but now felt depressing. *Maybe it's just my mood.*

Had it really been two years since we last saw Helen? I remember sitting at one of the tables, watching the carp swim along the maze of waterways threaded throughout the ground floor, free drinks in hand from the manager's daily Happy Hour. The smell of popcorn filled the air and we laughed while crunching on the warm, fresh kernels, Alan making up stories about the giant koi and their endless search to find their way back to freedom. Glancing at it now, it all felt stale.

Unlocking the door to the suite, I dropped my purse on the writing table in the living room before wheeling my bag into the adjacent bedroom, grateful to the hotel staff for allowing me such an early check-in. *I'll unpack later; right now I need to stay focused on my to-do list.* I settled onto the sagging couch, found my cell phone, and dialed

Alan's number. As I waited for him to answer I pictured him fumbling in his pocket to find his phone and rushing to push the talk button before it went to voicemail.

"Hey, hi! How are you? Got in okay, I assume?" His voice was upbeat, in sharp contrast to my current state of mind.

"I'm here," I said, stating the obvious. "I still have no idea what I'm doing. I'm not completely sure where to even start. I've got the rest of today to get a plan in place before the shit hits the fan." I felt my anxiety creeping up and changed the subject. "How's everything going there?"

"It's all fine, mostly boring. I'm still in my meeting, but ducked out to answer your call. They've been talking about another re-org, but haven't really said much. Sean said he's been hearing more grumblings of possible layoffs, but at the moment I don't really care. Hell, I'd volunteer to go if they gave me a chance. Then I'd have some start-up money to get my own business going."

My stomach tightened. This wasn't where I wanted the conversation to go. Alan had hated his job for the past year, and it hadn't been much better for several years before that. He still loved working with computers and software, but the bureaucracy of a large company, the endless meetings, and a series of frustrating managers impeding his ability to get things done, was wearing him down. We'd talked numerous times about him quitting and doing something on his own but we didn't have a plan, and leaping without a net wasn't my style. Now with everything going on with Helen, the last thing I needed to worry about was Alan's job. What I needed to do was calm down; Friday was looming and I had to be clear-headed.

"I'm sorry. I can't focus on this right now and every time you talk about quitting I get freaked. I shouldn't have asked. Let's tackle one thing at a time, and right now Helen's is the more urgent mess.

I need to be ready for tomorrow. I'll fill you in on my progress, assuming I'm still awake when you get here tonight."

I pulled out the list I'd composed on the way down and began organizing my day. Talk to Myron; meet the neighbor and get more information; breathe. I'd already set up a time to meet with the social worker and dealt with the conference folks while awaiting my flight. As expected, it was too late for a refund.

Rummaging through my shoulder bag, I found Myron's number on a pad of paper tucked in alongside my computer. *May as well start with the most onerous task first.* I picked up the phone and punched the numbers, almost hoping he wouldn't answer. But on the third ring his voice came through.

"Hello, this is Myron. Whom may I ask is calling?" His voice was as stiff and formal as his words.

"Hi, Myron, it's Shelly, again, Helen's step-granddaughter. I just got here and checked into the hotel. As I explained yesterday, I need to get a better grasp of what's going on so I can help her when you take Bruce. This has all been quite a shock and we both know it will be devastating for her. She'll be very confused. Hell, I'm confused." I restrained myself from saying more, hoping to elicit an ounce of compassion where so far I'd seen none. "I think it would help for us to talk more."

"Well, now is as good a time as any. I've already spoken with Kim, the social worker, and have things under control on my end. If you and Kim can figure out how to handle Helen, I'll do my best to help, although my focus will be on getting Dad taken care of safely." His voice softened a bit.

"Okay, I can do that. But can you fill me in a little more? You have to understand this is really coming out of nowhere for me. I talk to Helen regularly and other than complaints of being tired, not being able to drive, and your dad's many medical appointments, she sounds normal to me. I've obviously been missing something."

Myron exhaled slowly. I sensed he was trying to figure out where to start. He'd witnessed the changes up close, and they must have been going on for quite a while. Once again I wondered how I hadn't put together the significance of Helen's lapses. *But I hadn't been looking for anything to be wrong.* Helen's explanations of exhaustion had made sense without any contradicting context.

"Here's the deal: Helen hasn't been feeding Dad, and at his age he's too frail to take care of himself. He's been begging me to get him out, but he also was worried about what would happen to her." They had spent eleven lovely years together.

"It started slowly," he continued. "She'd forget where she put things, and start fussing at Dad. He'd calm her down and help her search. Then they had the accident." I remembered Helen's panic when she hydroplaned the old Chrysler in a deluge, skidding across an intersection and crashing into an oak tree. Luckily, she hadn't been going fast, and Bruce only suffered bruised ribs. He spent a night in the hospital, but that was only to make sure that at his age there weren't any internal injuries. The car had been totaled, and Helen's natural aversion to driving, in addition to Bruce discouraging her purchasing a replacement vehicle combined to restrict her freedom. Upon reflection, the loss of the car seemed to coincide with the increase in Helen's complaints.

"At first, after the car was gone, she'd call a taxi to drive her into San Toro for her errands. Despite the hassle and expense of the cab, she and Dad would make an outing out of it, seeing friends or attending one of his club events. I'd come down once a week to take him to lunch, and sometimes I dropped Helen off at the supermarket to shop while he and I visited. It worked fine for a while, and then I noticed she took longer and longer to do the simplest things. Dad and I would have finished lunch and be sitting

32

in the parking lot, and she still wasn't done. Once I found her standing in front of the meat counter. She looked completely lost and confused. But when I called to her, she fussed and wondered why I was there. That happened more and more often. Over the same time I noticed Dad was losing weight. You know how thin he is to begin with, and with his advanced age I got worried. After a lot of prodding, he admitted that Helen was forgetting to cook his meals. She'd talk about making dinner, and head out to the kitchen, but soon she'd be back and nothing was done. She'd repeat the conversation, go back down the hall, and still no food." He paused, showing the first hint of emotion I'd seen. "He doesn't want to leave, but he knows he needs better care. He's worried about her, but his need for self-preservation is stronger. He didn't know what to do, so I finally made the decision for him."

I simply listened. It was hard to recognize the person Myron described, but it filled in some gaps in a few of my more recent experiences. Helen had been the epitome of organization. She'd staged dinner parties for dozens, juggling drink orders with full course meals, a whir of activity while also making sure everyone was comfortable and well tended to. She'd pulled off a surprise birthday party for Papa Paul's eightieth, planning it a full year in advance knowing they'd be in Europe for the two months leading up to the big day. His complete bewilderment when the crowd yelled 'Happy Birthday' proved her prowess at keeping a secret. Even after his death she kept the house in excellent condition, putting the gardeners to shame with her enthusiasm, pulling weeds and rearranging plants when the mood struck or the need arose. Her energy was boundless. Her efficiency was legendary. When had it slipped?

"I tried to talk them both into going into a retirement home. Dad was willing but Helen refused. He wouldn't go without her, and no amount of pleading would change her mind. At his suggestion I took them to visit a few, but she always had one objection or another: too expensive, too snooty, not enough space, too ornate. Clearly, she wasn't going to give in, and clearly he needed more care. I don't want to pull them apart, but she's left me no choice." The frustration was back in his voice.

"Thanks for telling me this. I had no idea it had become that bad. I get that this is what you need to do; what I also know is it won't be good for her." It was becoming apparent that Myron wasn't terribly fond of Helen, but he did accept that his father loved her, and it was obvious he didn't want her to suffer. He merely needed his dad to be okay.

"I'll coordinate with Kim and let you know if anything changes, otherwise I'll see you at the house at ten tomorrow. Here's hoping for a miracle." I hung up the phone, leaned back on the couch, and closed my eyes. *What a mess. What a goddamned mess.*

After a few minutes I walked over to the tiny kitchenette and measured a cup of water into the small coffee maker, added the packet and pushed the 'on' button. I welcomed the mindless activity before I had to tackle the next item on my to-do list.

Next up was calling Molly, the neighbor. I hoped we could meet in her home so I could get a quick glimpse of Helen's house. I wasn't sure what I'd learn, but it might give me a hint as to what was going on. I also wanted to pick her brain for more insight into what she'd been noticing and, more importantly, wanted her aware of my plans in case I required any assistance the following day. I found her number in my notes, and was relieved when she agreed to have me come to the neighborhood. She mentioned how little Helen went out these days. I said I'd be there within the hour.

"There was a time when we'd sit in the front yard watching the twins play while chatting about neighborhood gossip. She always enjoyed knowing what was happening on the street, but that was another of the changes I've noticed: her interest in what's going on around her has greatly diminished. In this instance, that's probably a good thing; I doubt she'll recognize the rental car, or if she does, she won't realize it's you driving."

I gathered my scattered papers and folded them neatly before stuffing them into my purse. The coffee maker was silent, indicating its job was done. I mixed in the creamer and sweetener and sipped the dismal concoction while deciding what to take for the day. The forecast was for the mid seventies so no need for a jacket. I was meeting with the social worker later that afternoon and wanted a legal pad for notes, so I grabbed it along with my purse. Finishing the last of the coffee I tossed the cup into the nearby wastebasket, picked up the room key, turned off the living room light, and headed out.

Chapter 4

The street was quiet as I pulled up just past Helen's house. The privacy hedge they'd planted years before blocked any view out her front windows and I felt reasonably discreet as I stepped out of the car and walked to Molly's front door. A petite blonde in her mid-thirties in jeans and a *San Toro Elementary School Parent* t-shirt answered my knock within seconds.

"Hi, you must be Shelly. I'm Molly. I was keeping an eye out for you. Come on in," she said without hesitation, closing the door behind me. "Nice to put a face to the name. Helen talked about you quite often."

I glanced around, always curious to see how different families had upgraded the houses in the neighborhood over time. This was clearly a home filled with the active five-year old twins Helen often mentioned. Toys were stacked in corners and on shelves, and a LEGO spaceship of some kind was being constructed on the coffee table. Pieces were strewn all over, the evidence of a work still in progress. Children's books were scattered around the room. It had a lived in, comfortable feeling.

"Your place reminds me of what it was like when my kids were little; the perfect mix of chaos and organization. I love it," I said. I liked Molly instantly.

"Want something to drink? Coffee, tea, water?" She moved toward the kitchen as she talked. "I'd offer a glass of wine but the twins get dropped off from kindergarten in an hour. Not good to smell of alcohol this early," she laughed.

"I'll probably need a bottle by tomorrow night, but for now I'll take water. I had some really crappy coffee at the hotel so I'm good." I retreated to the couch, picking up a stray LEGO and placing it on the table, glad to have seen it before finding it when it poked me. "So what's been going on? This is all bizarre."

Molly handed me a glass of water and took a sip of her own before speaking. "Helen's a delight, and her joy in playing with the twins has been such a gift for us. Since Jon's parents live in Germany, and mine are on the East Coast, she's filled in as kind of a surrogate grandmother. The kids adore her and she loves to fuss over them. It's been a nice relationship over the past couple of years. We'd have a cup of coffee, talk about our gardens, the neighborhood; you know, simple things. But in the last few months she seemed more agitated. She complained about Bruce, about being tired, about a lot of little things. It wasn't like her, but I figured it was a normal part of aging."

Molly paused. I sensed she was still unsure if she had violated Helen's privacy. I nodded for her to continue.

"Bruce's health has been declining; his skin cancer's spread, which means more doctor appointments. But without a car, getting to those appointments became another challenge. Once in awhile I was able to give them a lift, but with the kids my time's pretty booked up. I don't know when I realized she wasn't eating much. She may have mentioned something, but recently I began to put two and two together and started getting concerned. That's when I remembered I had your number and called."

"I'm glad you did. Turns out a lot more has been going on, and as you know, a lot more is about to happen. If you hadn't reached out, it would have been a disaster." I filled Molly in on Myron's plan to take Bruce without notice.

"Are you friggin' kidding me?" Molly was as stunned as I had been. "How in the world did he think Helen would handle this? What does he think will happen to her?" In her growing anger she stumbled on her words. "I can't imagine this. What are you going to do?"

"I'm not exactly sure, although I know I need to be here when Myron arrives. She can't be alone." That much had been clear all along. "I think my husband, Alan, and I will show up at the same time Myron does, pretending we just happen to be coming by for a visit. Maybe in the confusion she won't question it, especially if she's as bad as everyone says."

I didn't know how Molly might help, but it would be reassuring to see a friendly face if everything went to hell. "Will you be home tomorrow around ten? That's when Myron's supposed to be there."

Molly smiled, "I'll be here. The kids will be in school and, of course, I'll do whatever you need. Let me know."

Taking a last sip of water, I stood to leave. "I can't tell you how much better it feels to have someone to talk to who knows them. Knowing you care about Helen makes it a little easier for me. I'll keep you posted." Gathering my things, I glanced out at the house across the street before opening the door. "Her place looks so normal," I said softly. "You'd never guess it was all falling apart on the inside."

I sat in the car staring at the home my grandparents had lived in for over forty years. They were among the first purchasers in a tract development built in the early '60s and fell in love with the area and its moderate climate. So much of the Bay Area was subjected to the chilling fog that crept over the coastal mountains in the afternoons, but their corner of San Toro was somehow protected. One of Helen's favorite sayings was that they had 'died and gone to heaven' when they came west and discovered the then-quaint town.

The house hadn't changed much since they first moved in other than modifications to the outside as their entertaining needs evolved. Built on the hillier side of the block, the garage was at street level with steps leading up to the front door. Aluminum siding covered what had been wood, the result of a shrewd salesman in the '70s who convinced them they'd never have to repair it again. Rocks filled most of the yard spaces, a consequence of a severe drought sometime before Papa Paul's death. The house was still painted a pale yellow, one of Helen's favorite colors, although it had faded. The white trim showed signs of neglect, too, as did the metal stair railing. The interior was probably in similar need of attention; they'd never upgraded the kitchens or bathrooms; their priorities had been travelling and remaining financially solvent, not keeping up with the latest decorator trends.

They'd been so happy there. I thought of the hundreds of friends they'd made, becoming involved in various service organizations, and entertaining in their modest but welcoming home. Even after Papa Paul's death, Helen refused to relocate anywhere else, despite our best efforts to get her to move closer to us. Meeting Bruce, and his subsequent move into her home, really had been a lifesaver for her, allowing her to remain comfortably in familiar surroundings. And while their social circle slowly diminished with his advancing age and the increasing impact of his skin cancer, they were happy together and happy at home. She'd been in that house longer than anywhere else she'd lived.

I couldn't imagine staying anywhere that long, or what it would be like to leave such a place if I had. Fourteen years had been the longest I'd lived anywhere. It was all too much to even contemplate at the moment.

I mulled over my conversations with Myron and Molly as I started the car and pulled away, driving back through streets that were so recognizable after all the years visiting. Putting together what I'd learned, it was obvious that something was quite off. There had always been so much focus on Papa Paul that I knew little of Helen's family health history. It had never come up in our conversations. I had spoken with Papa Paul about her, but only in regards to his inevitable passing.

"I worry about Helen when I'm gone," he'd shared with me numerous times in his later years. "I don't know how she'll handle being alone, being without me. She's always been prone to depression, and if she falls apart I seriously wonder if she'll take her own life. I need to know you'll be there for her, take care of her." It was easy to make that promise to him, to be the one he depended on to watch over his beloved wife. But in all those conversations neither of us suspected it would be her mind that would falter.

I thought about the weekend I spent with Helen at the hospital when Papa Paul was dying. She opened up in a way she never had, filling in much about her childhood that I suspected had previously been known only to Papa Paul. Her sharing felt urgent, as if she needed someone to keep her stories. I realized he'd been the only one who held them for her for all those years, and his protectiveness made even more sense to me once I understood her history. She'd found love and acceptance with him, but I wondered if she ever truly healed from some of the more painful experiences she'd had in her life. That night brought us even closer, and I think Papa Paul sensed it as well: he slipped peacefully away almost at the moment Helen told me her final secret.

And now his concerns were real: she wasn't doing well, not from the depression he had feared, but from an unexpected direction. Her mind was slipping, although I still had no idea why. What was clear was my promise to him: I would do whatever was necessary to make sure Helen was taken care of.

Chapter 5

Kim and I had arranged to meet at a coffee shop near downtown San Toro at 2 o'clock. Finding parking in the small strip mall was always a challenge, but for once in the last twenty-four hours luck was on my side. As I pulled into the lot, an elderly man walked out of the neighboring dry cleaners. I signaled my intent and waited, tapping my fingers impatiently on the steering wheel while he got into his car, adjusted his seat belt, and started the engine. I watched while he backed out, making sure to give him plenty of room, and then gently eased my rental car into the tiny space he'd just vacated. Locking the door, I slid through the narrow gap between cars and crossed the parking lot, looking through the windows of the Starbucks as I approached the entrance. The shop was only half full, not quite time for the mid-afternoon caffeine replenishment rush. I pulled open the door and glanced around, zeroing in on the woman seated alone at a round metal table in the corner. A small array of brochures and folders gave her away as the person I was seeking.

"You must be Kim?" I asked as the woman rose to greet me. "Hi, I'm Shelly Johnson." I smiled, extending my hand.

"It's nice to meet you. I'm sorry it's under these circumstances," Kim responded, taking my hand in hers.

I sighed. "Yeah, thanks for getting together. I've never dealt with a situation like this, especially a thousand miles from my comfort zone. I'm not even sure what questions to ask you." I pulled out a chair and sat, relieved to be able to dump everything on what I hoped was a knowledgeable professional. "I'm a therapist, but it's all been in private practice for the past twenty-plus years. I haven't done much on the social work side of things since leaving an institutional setting early in my career."

"I get that. Hopefully I can give you some information that might answer some of your questions, although I'm not a hundred percent sure what Myron is expecting me to do or exactly what I'm walking into myself." Kim shuffled her papers and glanced at her notes.

'Here's what I know so far: I'll be there with Myron when Bruce tells Helen he's moving into the nursing home. Myron thought I could talk to her while he packs Bruce's bag and gets him out to the car, that I could offer her some of the services the county has available."

I stared at her. "Is he f'ing serious? He's too afraid to tell her up front so he thinks she'll just sit down with a total stranger to look over brochures while he takes Bruce away from the house? He's out of his f'ing mind if he believes for a second that she won't put up a fight. I think he wants you there to alleviate his guilt about leaving Helen alone." Anger flooded me and I had to pause to gather myself; it wasn't helpful and it wasn't Kim's fault. Yelling at her wouldn't get us anywhere.

"I need a drink." I stood up before Kim could say anything. "Can I get you something?"

"A tall Earl Grey tea would be fine; a splash of cream. Thanks," she replied. "That'll give me a few minutes to organize my thoughts. But it's rather obvious I need more information than what Myron passed on."

I walked to the counter and placed an order for a chai latte and Kim's tea, the brief interruption helping to calm my thoughts.

Drinks in hand, I returned to the table, sat down and took a sip of the warm spiced tea. At least that was familiar; everything else seemed completely off-kilter. Kim popped the top off her cup and stirred her drink for a moment before removing the tea bag and setting it on the up-ended lid. Leaving it to cool for a minute, she sat quietly, waiting for me to talk.

"Clearly there's a lot of background you don't have. I don't know what will be helpful for you, so tell me, where do we begin?"

"Well, I only got the basics from Myron, mostly details like her full name and age for some preliminary paperwork. Why don't you tell me about Helen, and what you know of her current living conditions. Then I'll ask questions." Her voice was reassuring. I knew the tone all too well, having used it myself with distraught clients, tempering their anxieties with my knowledge, their panic with my calm. It was both comforting and a bit disconcerting to have the tables turned.

"I haven't seen her yet this trip and before that it's been well over a year. We talk on the phone, but obviously I've missed some big clues. The thought of some sort of dementia, or whatever is going on, never crossed my mind." For the next fifteen minutes I gave my perspective based on Molly and Myron's stories and my own recent phone conversations. I described Helen's personality and enough of her background to paint a portrait of a strong, kind, loving, and very stubborn woman who could also be prone to depression and bursts of anger. Kim listened, taking notes and occasionally interjecting with a question for clarification.

After I finished I leaned back in the chair. Now that Kim had all the information I wondered what advice she might offer. Hopefully it wouldn't just be handing over pamphlets and spouting platitudes.

"I'm glad you shared this with me. I think you're absolutely right that my showing up the way Myron had planned would be a disaster. You need to be the key player and my role will be to support you. What I can offer Helen will be minimal, but I can at least help get you information.

"For starters, I recommend you get her some kind of evaluation. I have the name of two neurologists in the area who see patients with dementia. Maybe you can set something up now to get the ball rolling. Do you have an attorney? Or does Helen? That's another person you'll need to speak with." She paused, glancing at her notes.

"Helen and my grandfather had one, who set up their Trust. After my grandfather died, I went to several of the meetings with her, because she knew I'd be in charge when she passed. I guess that's one piece of good news; she has everything legally in place. But I believe her attorney died a few years ago, so I'm going to have to find a new lawyer. I know she hasn't done that. I'll need some names if you have any, or let me know where to find someone decent." It felt better to be talking about concrete actions.

For the next twenty minutes we discussed names of lawyers and doctors, and the pros and cons of each. Reaching for my pen, I turned my notepad to a clean sheet, and copied down phone numbers and addresses, giving me plenty of places to start.

Chapter 6

The free glass of Happy Hour wine tasted remarkably good. I doubt it was a concerted effort on the part of the hotel to upgrade their offerings. It was more likely the much-appreciated effect of any alcohol after a crappy day. Too bad there wasn't a private hot tub somewhere surrounded by gently burning candles to go with it.

I'd spent the last few hours calling attorneys and medical offices. The first neurologist didn't have any openings for several weeks, but miraculously the second one had a cancellation on Monday and squeezed Helen in. One of the recommended attorneys could meet later in the week. I had to start somewhere, and there was some relief knowing a few ducks were lining up.

Finishing off the wine, I left a tip on the bar for the server and took the elevator back to my room on the fifth floor. The desire to run a warm bath, sip more wine, and soak away the cares of the day was tempting, but I had one more item on my to-do list: call my mother.

I felt my gut tighten as I looked for her number. She'd moved so often that I'd given up memorizing it, and was glad in this electronic age that all I had to do was delete and replace information instead of crossing out or trying to erase content in a paper address book. Every move was accompanied by the hope of 'this will be a good place for me; it'll be cheaper, better jobs, warmer, cooler, drier, not as dry'; the reasons were endless and the promises never fulfilled.

"Hi, Mom, how are you?" Might as well start with the lighter stuff first. "Sorry I haven't called for a few weeks, been really busy with work." It was only a bit of a stretch. We chatted a few minutes on safe topics before I veered the conversation to my grandmother.

"Mom, I need to let you know what's going on with Helen."

"Helen? Why, what's wrong? Is she sick or hurt?"

"I really don't know much, except no, I don't think she's hurt or ill." I paused a moment to gather my thoughts. I didn't want my irritation to come out in my voice. "I'll be seeing her tomorrow and will know more then. I just wanted to give you a head's up that things are kind of strange and I'm in San Toro to figure it all out." I gave her a brief outline of what I knew so far.

"Thanks for calling, and please keep me informed; I know you'll take care of everything. She's always trusted you." I barely listened as she went on, working to keep my thoughts in check. Maybe some part of her really did care how Helen was doing.

"Alan's coming tonight to help out and she really likes him. She's always going on about how much he reminds her of Papa Paul: 'he's so kind, he's so gentle,' you know, all the ways she'd describe Papa. And Alan's really good with her, listening to her stories, patient with her non-stop talking. Did I ever tell you what the kids said about Helen? They joked that she had HTD: hyperactive talking disorder. Helen cracked up when they told her. At least she knew she went on and on, and on and on."

I knew I was rambling, but it felt good to laugh about one of Helen's well-known characteristics. It took the focus off of the current situation and kept Mom from going off on one of her tangents, which, no matter how she phrased it, almost always included how tight money was, and if there was any way I might help her out. Despite having shared expenses with her roommate Julia for the past twenty years, she still couldn't manage her finances. They'd moved in together after Mom's last divorce and Julia's recent widowhood as a way to both combat loneliness and cut costs. But underlying everything was her jealousy that Papa Paul had provided for Helen instead of her, something she always denied if confronted, yet seeped into most conversations. I wasn't in the mood to hear any of it. I enjoyed our phone calls when they stayed light, and for those moments when they did I even felt close to her.

After a few more minutes of inconsequential talk we hung up. I fought the urge to go back to the bar for another glass of the house wine and instead went into the bathroom and turned on the tub. It wasn't a spa and candles, but it would still be relaxing to soak for a while. Alan wouldn't get in until around ten and I needed the break.

A half hour later, my mind and body finally calm, I stepped out of the tub, toweled off, and got into sweats. Settling onto the sofa, I picked up the TV remote and flicked through the channels until landing on a re-run of *The Simpsons*. It was just what I was looking for: something escapist until Alan arrived.

A gentle knock on the door was followed by the sound of the key card in the slot. I heard the click just before the heavy door cracked open and Alan's head poked in.

"Hey, you still awake?" His shoulder shoved the door wider, creating enough room for him to drag in a rolling bag stacked with his work backpack on top. "Sorry it's so late. I know you've had

49

quite the day. How was your mom?" He stood his suitcase against the desk and came over to the couch, bending down to give me a kiss.

"Mom was good, actually; I kept it brief and easy. Didn't give her an opening and hung up before it could get ugly. How was your trip? I'm so glad you're here." I'd already filled him in on most of the day's events while he was awaiting his flight from Seattle. "I don't want to spend any energy on her right now. I think I need a few minutes sitting here with you, just being quiet and together."

He sat down and put his arm around me as I nestled into him. "Just like this," I whispered.

Chapter 7

Sunlight streaming through the small gap in the curtains lit the room, and as I reached over to find Alan in the huge king size bed the anxieties of yesterday crept in. I lay in the stillness for a few moments, breathing deeply, reminding myself I could handle whatever came my way. Hadn't Mom always said I was the responsible and strong one in the face of difficulty? Resentment started to rise in my throat; I hated being put in that role, not because I feared responsibility, but because it always seemed to be paired with my mother abdicating it.

Pushing my emotions down, I reminded myself I wasn't alone; Alan was with me. We'd already weathered our share of challenges and only grown closer. I rolled over and gave him a good morning kiss, threw off the covers, and padded into the bathroom. This was not the time to fall apart. There was too much to be done.

What was also becoming apparent was that no matter what happened later it was clear Helen was going to need a lot more than hand-holding for a day or two. I felt a wave of exhaustion sweep over me.

"I wish I knew how she was going to take this," I told Alan over my vegetable omelet as we dined in the hotel's atrium restaurant.

"Not having seen her for so long it's hard to put together the stories we've heard from the Helen I know. My only hope is that she doesn't turn on us."

Alan nodded as he finished his toast. "If things are as bad as they say my guess is she'll welcome us being there. In the confusion she may not even question why we showed up."

"Aren't you ever the optimist? I'm foolishly hoping the same thing, but how could she not put it together? I just spoke to her about coming." I was still struggling to picture Helen as forgetful. "Okay, I think we've stalled as long as we could. It's time to head over and see what happens," the firmness of my statement covering the anxieties within as I pushed my chair away from the table and stood. "Let's get this over with."

Alan pulled the rental car up to the curb across the street from the house. Kim was already there, parked a little farther up the road. She came over when we stopped, and waited for me to get out. I took a deep breath and reached for the handle, pushing open the door and stepping onto the sidewalk. Alan came around from the driver's side and I made introductions. We waited, chatting quietly about last minute thoughts, until we saw Myron drive up and back his van into the driveway. He saw us gathered and nodded, acknowledging our presence as he turned and climbed the front stairs.

"Give him a few minutes to get inside and start things." My stomach was churning and my hands were shaking. All I could think about was Helen. Helen, who had no idea her entire world was about to be shattered.

I kept glancing at my watch while I paced the sidewalk. Alan stood quietly, his calm a balance against my nerves. I admired his ability to keep his attention on what we needed to accomplish, something I did easily with my clients and normally in my personal life, but not now when my emotions were so raw.

"Let's go, he's had enough time." Alan's voice broke through my thoughts. "She needs to see us, to know she's not alone." I knew he was right, but all I felt was dread. I turned to Kim and asked her to wait for five minutes before coming to the door. Too many people at once, especially a total stranger, would be more upsetting than helpful.

"Okay, I'm breathing, I'm ready." We walked up the stairs to the front door and rang the bell.

"Oh my God, I'm so glad you're here," Helen gushed as the door swung open. "Myron's here. He wants to take Bruce with him and Bruce says he wants to go. I don't believe him; he's never said anything to me. Why is he doing this to me?" Her words were tumbling out and I noticed tears flowing as I reached out to hold her. "Why is he taking him? What did I do? Why can't he stay?"

She kept repeating herself. I'd never seen her like this, not even when Papa Paul died. I glanced furtively at Alan for guidance. "What do I do?" I mouthed over Helen's head, as I held her tightly, afraid if I let her go she'd collapse in a heap. Alan nodded his head toward the street, suggesting we get her away from Myron and Bruce to let them escape unimpeded.

Shifting my hold on her, I put my arm around her shoulder and gently guided her down the front steps and out to the driveway. Helen's body was now shaking, her sobs gaining strength as she continued her recitation. "What did I do wrong? Why is he leaving?" I enfolded her in my arms again. It felt as if I was holding a wounded animal, not my feisty, in-control grandmother.

The sight of Bruce being helped down the stairs to Myron's waiting car triggered another strong reaction from Helen. Jerking away from me she rushed to his side, pleading with him. "Why do you want to go? Don't you want to be with me? Don't you love me? Why is Myron doing this?" Her begging and pleading was painful to witness and my anger was building. How the hell did Myron think he could take Bruce and leave her alone?

Fuck him. Fuck all of them. My rage was threatening to spew out, and I fought to contain myself. I'd be no help to Helen if I let my emotions out now. *Suck it up; take care of Helen,* I chanted silently as I moved toward the car and Bruce. I needed to hear him say he wanted out. It wasn't enough to hear it from Myron. Turning to Alan, I asked him to take Helen away from the car, hoping his presence would calm her enough for them to leave.

"Helen, say goodbye to Bruce. He's going with Myron now. We can figure it out later. Right now, come with me. Let's take a walk." He put his arm around Helen, gently but firmly pulling her away from the open car door. She hung onto Bruce, who urged her to listen to Alan. Reluctantly, she let go and allowed herself to be led toward the sidewalk before turning back to the car.

"Fine, leave. I don't care. Go with your son; let him take care of you. Get out now!" she yelled, a sudden bitterness in her voice. "Go! Get out!"

Her abrupt change in mood gave Alan the opening he needed. "Let's go over to Molly's. I think it'd be good to get away as well. You don't need to be here." Taking her arm, he steered her toward the street. Kim stood across the road, watching everything unfold. She kept her distance as they passed and went up Molly's walkway.

I went over to Bruce, who was settled into the front passenger seat of the car. He stared at the dashboard and began to speak. "I love Helen. I just need care she can't give. I need food. I need to eat." His face—half gone from all the surgeries to control the ravages of skin cancer caused by years of sailing—was flat. His eyes avoided looking up at me as his voice, almost inaudible, continued. "She can't remember to cook for me. She wants to take care of me, but I don't think she can anymore. Please take care of her; she's a wonderful woman." His words conveyed his sadness, but they felt empty, exhausted. He'd given up; he was leaving. He couldn't save her.

"We'll arrange for Myron to pick up the rest of your stuff. Good luck," was all I could muster. I, too, just wanted them gone.

Kim crossed the street to stand with me as Myron pulled out and we watched them drive away.

"You were right, he had no clue," she said softly. 'This would have been a disaster and so hurtful to Helen. I'm glad you warned me."

"Bruce looks so frail and pitiful. He really does need something Helen can't provide. I just wish there was a better way to have handled it. Now I get to pick up the pieces, and I can tell it's not going to be easy. She's not the Helen I remember at all. She was devastated when my grandfather died, and she was more together then. If her memory is really going, how is she going to figure this out?"

"You'll be here to help her. But it's obvious she doesn't need to meet me right now, if ever," Kim replied. "Why don't you call me later and we can talk once you have a better idea how I can really be of service to you. Whatever you need, just let me know." She gave me a hug.

"It's good to know I have your support. I'm sure I'll be calling you." I said as we walked across the street. Kim headed to her car and I went once again to Molly's front door. This time I didn't bother to wait for anyone to answer my knock. I turned the knob, and pushing the door gently, let myself in.

Helen and Alan were sitting together on the couch, his arm around her as he spoke quietly and stroked her short gray hair, comforting her as he would a frightened child. "You took fantastic care of Bruce; he was lucky to have you for so long," he reassured her over and over.

I came over and sat on Helen's other side, taking her free hand in both of mine. Her skin felt soft and fragile, and she seemed much older than the last time we'd visited. She'd always been tiny, but next to Alan she seemed smaller, a shrunken version of her usual powerhouse self. Even long after Papa Paul died, I remembered Helen demonstrating her fitness skills, taking great pride in the squats, burpees, and push-ups she had done every day since she was in nursing school. She loved patting her stomach, bragging that even in her eighties she retained the flat shape of her youth. Of course, she'd always add, laughing, that included her chest, 'flat as a pancake!'

Seeing her so vulnerable brought me to the verge of tears. "Alan's right, Helen; Bruce was fortunate to have you taking care of him for so long. He's just so old now, he needs more care. It's not that he doesn't love you, he told me that before he left." I hoped my words would not only help Helen, but also me.

"I'm so glad you're here. What would I do without you?" She took turns looking at us. "Did I know you were coming? Oh, I'm so glad you're here," she went on before we could answer.

"Why did he want to leave? Wasn't I taking good care of him? That awful son, it's Myron's fault. He made him go. I know he wouldn't have gone if he hadn't insisted," she continued, moving rapidly between anguish and anger. I didn't know which was better. For the moment it seemed best to simply sit and bear witness to her mood swings, offering agreement and reassurances wherever possible.

"I knew you were coming, I just forgot. You know how hard it's been taking care of Bruce, I get tired and just don't remember everything." While her explanation seemed plausible, it wasn't true. Helen didn't know we were coming; in fact, she'd explicitly told me not to visit. Was she really that confused or had the events of the last hour muddled her mind?

"I'm sorry I forgot you were coming today. I've just been so busy taking care of Bruce and I'm so tired," Helen's eyes searched out mine, looking for understanding.

"It's okay, Helen, I know how tired you've been," I said quietly and patted her hand. "It's a lot that you've had to do, especially without a car."

"Myron is mean, taking Bruce like this. Bruce didn't want to go; Myron made this all up." Helen's voice was bitter and angry, the shift in mood as abrupt as the stiffening in her body. "He's always been cold, so cold. But he's Bruce's son and I had to be nice to him. But he's a cold, cold man."

"Well, you won't have to deal with him anymore." I attempted to calm Helen down. "What he did was cruel and now you won't have to see him. You were very good to Bruce and we all know that."

"I can't believe Bruce wanted to go. What did I do wrong? Why would he leave me like this? Wasn't I enough?" The wailing returned, along with deep, racking sobs.

Alan looked over at me, mouthing silently, 'What in the hell do we do now?' I shrugged, and whispered back, "Just sit with her, I guess?" Neither of us knew what else to do. Helen was clearly distraught, asking the same questions over and over as if each utterance was the first time. Something felt very different than simply listening to an emotional woman in shock, processing her grief. She had no memory of covering the same ground only minutes before.

Molly kindly busied herself with chores around the house, discreetly offering an occasional glass of water as she moved from room to room, giving us privacy to help Helen settle down. The conversations cycled over the same subjects, with the two of us offering the same reassurances until she was exhausted. It was time to leave.

"I'm hungry, let's go get some lunch. How about we go into San Toro and find some food?" I suggested, hoping that staying away from the house longer would distract Helen, giving everyone a temporary break and a chance to regroup. At least we could try and get some food in her; she seemed frail enough that we didn't want her getting sick from lack of nutrition. It was clear that Bruce wasn't the only one who hadn't been eating.

Chapter 8

The short drive into San Toro was an emotional and conversational roller coaster. Helen's focus ping-ponged from Bruce to complaints about increasing traffic to stories about the changes to the shopping center we passed. Her mood was equally all over the place: happily chatting about nothing, surprise that we were visiting, anger at Bruce, followed by a flood of tears. Her anger evoked the fierceness I'd witnessed on a few prior occasions, but the tears brought out a quality I'd never seen, not even when Papa Paul died. She seemed so lost and vulnerable.

Pulling into one of the parking garages off the main street in town, Alan found a spot not far from the entrance. He jumped out of the driver's seat and scooted around to open her door, take her hand, and help her out.

"Let's find someplace to eat," he said as he guided her gently toward the sidewalk. "Is there a place you prefer?" he asked, hoping by engaging her she'd focus on the task and not on her loss, even if only for a few moments.

"Oh, I don't care, anyplace is fine." She shook her head. "You pick something you like."

I came up alongside Helen and took her other hand. "How about that restaurant across the street? It looks like a pleasant place." I sensed that asking her to make a decision was too much, and it was more important to keep things light and moving than to find the perfect cafe to grab a bite.

As we settled into the booth I glanced at my watch. It had been almost six hours since breakfast; four since we'd arrived on Helen's doorstep. The day was barely half over and I was already worn out. It had become clear to me, and I assume to Alan as well, that we'd be staying at Helen's tonight. There was no way we could leave her alone. I only hoped that the trauma of this morning would mean sleep tonight. I sighed quietly and opened the menu.

Watching us pack our bags and check out of the hotel kept Helen occupied for part of the afternoon, but we could only avoid going to the house for so long. She'd calmed down somewhat during lunch, but as we turned into the familiar neighborhood her questions and tears returned, replaced by a raging anger when we climbed the steps and opened the front door. She walked through the rooms of the small rambler pulling items off shelves and out of drawers.

"This is Bruce's, get it out of here!" she yelled. "He doesn't want to be here, then get his stuff out of here, too! Why didn't Myron take it when he took his father? I don't want it, I don't want his things!" Her yelling continued as we followed her. "Why does he think I want his papers when he isn't here?" she screamed as she swept a pile of files off the desk and onto the floor.

"Helen, it's okay, we'll pack it up and send it to him. You don't need to do anything. Just tell us what's his and we'll take care of it for you." I kept my voice calm in stark contrast to Helen's venomous commentary. "Alan and I can do it. We'll find some boxes and get it all packed. We can arrange to have it picked up, so you don't have to deal with Myron; we can do that." My reassurances weren't having much of an effect.

"Alan, why don't you and Helen look for something to pack this stuff in?" I asked, hoping the distraction might help.

"Helen, come with me, help me find some boxes. Do you have any in the garage?" he said as if redirecting a toddler who had thrown a temper tantrum. "Let's go look." Remarkably, she quieted and allowed him to guide her out of the office. I stayed behind, picking up the papers and stacking them back on the desk that had once been Papa Paul's and was now filled with Bruce's unique collection of odds and ends. I glanced around at the walls that had previously been filled with signed photos of politicians and astronauts, a collection of campaign pins and buttons, and a silly pseudo Latin poster I'd always been proud to decode every time I visited as a young child:

osi billi si ergo.

fortibuses in ero.

no billi demis trux.

sewatis enim?

cowsin dux!

Like Papa Paul, it was no longer there. In its place was a photo of a sailing ship; in fact, the room was filled with souvenirs that were all foreign. Bruce's passion was the sea. He had owned or crewed on various sailboats throughout his life, including racing in the first Trans-Pac after the war, and had only retired from boats when his skin cancer forced him into the shade and onto land. The furniture in the room was the same, but it had been claimed, and now abandoned, by Bruce.

Alan greeted me as I returned to the living room. "We found a few boxes, and I've asked Helen to point out some of Bruce's things as a start. We can find more tomorrow and keep packing. The sooner his effects are gone perhaps the sooner Helen will find peace in her home; no constant reminders."

The thought was comforting. "Where is she? What's she doing now?" I whispered, not sure if Helen was around the corner, listening.

"She's still in the garage. It's crammed full of newspapers. Apparently one of her neighbors asked her to save them while they were out of town, but there's more than two months' worth down there. No one in their right mind would have asked her to do that! What in the hell is going on?" The incredulity in his voice wasn't lost on me.

"I have no friggin' idea. I think we just have to keep focused, get Bruce's stuff out, and figure it out as we go. Let's start in the office where I can tell what's his."

We spent the next two hours packing what we could into the boxes we found, along with a suitcase Helen said was his. While we sorted, we listened to her vacillate between teary-eyed reminiscing and cold hatred. Her hurt was painful to witness; keeping busy helped along with hugs and reassurances that she had been good to him and it wasn't her fault he had to go.

When we brought home leftovers from lunch to re-heat for a simple dinner, I was startled to find the refrigerator crammed full with mostly rotting food, along with several tubs of butter spread, all unused. The freezer was jammed as well, this time with packages of vegetables, most of the same variety and all unopened. What did it all mean? There was clearly plenty of food to cook, but none of it was being used. Why so many duplicates? There's no way they could have eaten it all, and no way they needed this much food. Another mystery that needed to be solved, but not before we ate and had a good night's sleep.

Chapter 9

We awoke to the light coming between the slats of the old mini-blinds. We'd slept on the trundle bed, which when pulled out consumed most of the tiny room, leaving only a small sliver of space for our bags. Moving around was a challenge.

The house was quiet. "Let's see if she's up yet. I don't hear anything but I'm not sure we will." I whispered. "I hope she slept; she certainly was exhausted."

After throwing on our clothes from the day before, we headed down the hall toward the kitchen when Alan suddenly veered off into the living room. He grabbed my arm and silently beckoned me to follow him.

"I packed these last night, didn't I?" he whispered, staring at the empty cardboard boxes on the floor. "I put the things Helen told me to into them, right?" his incredulity inflected in his voice. "I'm not imaging things, am I?"

I stared. The boxes were full when we went to bed, and now there wasn't a shred of evidence that we had packed anything. All the trinkets, mementos, and papers were gone, not a trace of any of them to be seen. The boxes sat neatly on the floor, empty. I glanced around the room. On the mantle sat the small ship in a bottle I knew I had wrapped in newsprint and placed in the box. The silver flask Helen had said was Bruce's favorite was back on the side table, as was the oversized photo album of his last yacht. We looked at each other. What happened?

We walked into the kitchen, stunned. Helen was sitting at her usual seat, her back to us. She seemed oblivious to what was happening, reading the paper and sipping her coffee as if nothing was out of the ordinary.

"Good morning, Helen," I smiled and kissed her gently on the cheek. "How was your night?"

"Oh, I don't sleep much, I never do. I got up and straightened the house a bit, did some chores. I really don't need much sleep. Have you had breakfast yet?" she went on as if this were a regular visit. I wondered if she even knew she had put Bruce's stuff away, or for that matter, if she even remembered the events of yesterday. "I have cereal; it's what I have every morning. I can make coffee if you'd like, or tea. I still have that electric hot pot you gave me for Christmas when mine broke. I remember how hard I looked for one I liked and couldn't find one anywhere. I was so pleased when you sent me one."

I was taken aback by Helen's clear memory of something that had happened several years before. This was the grandmother I knew, the one who never forgot anything, who kept things running smoothly. Maybe Myron was mistaken; maybe he had another reason for taking his father away that had nothing to do with her forgetfulness.

"Where's Bruce?" Helen's voice interjected. "Did Myron come and get him this morning for an appointment?"

As quickly as my hopes had risen, they were dashed. How could she not remember where he'd gone after all the crying, anger, and conversations of the past twenty-four hours?

"Helen, Myron came yesterday morning and moved Bruce to a nursing home. Bruce needed more care because of his health," I spoke quietly as I put her arm around her. "He didn't want to leave, but he had to go."

"Of course I remember, I was just confused for a moment. That nasty Myron, he's always been so cold, so cruel. He does whatever he wants. I bet he's doing it to get Bruce's money." She flipped instantly into anger and bitterness; the sweet, gentle Helen was gone. "Well, fine, be done with them. I don't want anything to do with either one of them. How ungrateful after all the years I took care of Bruce. It wasn't all fun, you know; he was constantly going to doctors and couldn't do things like when we first met. I had to drive him everywhere and believe me it wasn't easy." She showed no sign of slowing down.

"Helen, can you show me where the cereal is?" Alan interrupted, hoping to divert her attention. "I can find the milk and I guess bowls are up here, but I can't find the cereal." He opened cabinets and drawers, pulling out dishes and utensils and setting them on the counter.

"In the bread box," I pointed. "Over there, same side as the sink."

"I think they're crisper if I keep them in there," Helen said, rushing over to open the door to the ancient metal box sitting in the corner near the stovetop. "I have bran and some Rice Krispies. Bruce likes Rice Krispies but I have to give him bran to... you know... keep him regular." She chattered away, bustling about as she grabbed a cereal box and several plastic bags held together with twist ties. "I make sure to give him a quarter cup every morning."

Helen had always offered far more information than needed, and talked faster and with more details than anyone I knew. Ask her a question about the new paint color on the house across the street and before you could stop her she'd launch into a story about the woman's husband's cousin's third nephew who was in the Navy and met a girl in Australia who grew up near a small town outside Sydney and when they visited Australia they went to the Opera House and met someone who used to live in California and by then whoever asked the question was completely lost. Somehow she always came back to the original story, but by then no one cared.

While I was happy to keep her occupied, I wasn't prepared for one of her tangential meanderings this early in the day. "Thanks, Helen. I'd love a cup of tea," hoping the shift in subject would stop the digression into a discussion of Bruce's bowels. "Why don't you fill the pot while I get the tea bags." I'd been coming to this house for over forty years, and very little had changed, including the location of the tea in the upper cabinet next to the fridge, which was also where she kept her stash of chocolates. Her admitted chocoholism made Christmas shopping simple over the past many years. Easy to send, always appreciated, and didn't add to an accumulation of more stuff she clearly didn't need. Plus it was nice to sneak some pieces when I visited and had an urge for something sweet. Reaching for the box of Earl Grey tea, I was comforted to see a bag of Snickers stuffed into the crammed space; thankfully, some things were the same.

We sat at the dining table, conversing pleasantly about food preferences and Alan's avoidance of oats, feeling a need to explain his reason for declining her insistent offer to buy Cheerios in case he didn't want the Rice Krispies. How his body rebelled from breathing in the heavily saturated dust after shoveling three loads of oats from the grain bin into the truck on the family farm. Unlike Helen, though, he avoided describing exactly how they affected him. I intermingled stories of Papa Paul, who had also grown up on a farm, but in New Hampshire, many I'd heard him tell and others from his autobiography. His detailed descriptions of life covering almost an entire century had fascinated me. Over the next half hour we enjoyed breakfast while Helen added stories of her own, and for a short while, Bruce was forgotten.

"We need to pack up Bruce's things. I don't want them here," she announced as we finished cleaning up the last of the dishes. "If he doesn't want to be here then I don't want his stuff." She burst into tears. "Why did he go? Wasn't I good enough? What did I do wrong?" I sighed. It was going to be another long day.

Alan spent part of the morning in town, finding a package store that sold boxes to supplement the few he'd found in the garage. We certainly had plenty of newspapers for filler; no sense in wasting money on bubble wrap. Once again Helen directed us as we carefully placed each item into a box, taped it shut, wrote Bruce's name on it, and carried it down the stairs to await pickup. Alan stacked them carefully in a row, along with the few small items of furniture that Helen indicated were his. Her mood fluctuated throughout the day, angry one minute, tearful the next, but she was determined to rid the house of any traces of him. We were grateful for the commotion of packing.

We stopped late in the afternoon, then hopped in the car to drive over to the local marina. We strolled along the waterfront, watching the sun as it descended toward the horizon. Afterward we went into the shabby-looking seafood restaurant nestled in the far corner of the lot, a diner we had often frequented when I visited my grandparents as a young girl. It was one of those funky places that had never been updated, but I remembered the food being delicious and wasn't disappointed.

Sitting in our bedroom later that night—Helen's door closed and hopefully asleep—we strategized our next steps. I had clients lined up starting Monday. It was obvious I had to cancel, but for how long? A week, two weeks, what? Every hour missed was money lost as well as continuity for those who depended on their appointments.

"I guess I plan it a week at a time,' I said quietly. "Email my clients and let them know we had a family emergency. I'll re-schedule them for the following week and see how it goes. I hate being so damn vague but I don't know what else to do." That felt better than being open ended. I didn't want to stay in San Toro any longer than necessary.

"Why don't I fly home as planned, take care of some things at work and at the house, and then come back later in the week if it looks like you'll still be here?" Alan's idea made sense, although I hated the thought of him leaving so soon. The reality was there wasn't much for him to do. I could handle doctors and meetings with lawyers. We didn't both have to do it.

"I'll call the airlines tomorrow. I'll have to find a place where there's better cell coverage. It sucks here." Helen had a landline, but there was little privacy for talking. The house was too small and the walls too thin. "Thankfully, Molly's Internet is strong and she was willing to share her password. I'd go nuts without some contact to the outside world."

A plan in place, we settled down in the trundle bed, the twin mattresses scrunched as closely together as possible, but it still felt odd to be in separate spaces. It took a long time to finally nod off, and despite my need for sleep it was a fitful night. I doubted Alan's was much better.

Chapter 10

"Shelly, come here," Alan whispered from the doorway of the tiny bedroom. "Please tell me I'm not crazy," he said as he turned away. "Please tell me we packed all of this yesterday and carried it downstairs. I don't f'ing believe it! What the hell is going on?"

I was shocked. Everything was back where it had been. When had Helen had the time to unpack the boxes? How had she managed to carry all the items back upstairs, and even more importantly, why? We went into the garage. The boxes, full and taped shut last night, sat opened and empty on the floor. The newspapers were once again stacked as high as they had been. Alan opened the side door and peered into the recycling bin: empty. How were we ever going to make progress if she undid everything while we slept?

"I have no idea," was all I could muster. "I don't get it. I wonder if she wakes up at night and can't remember that he's not here. It must freak her out that his stuff is packed up. But why wouldn't she simply realize he's not in her bed? Where would she think he'd gone?"

"I'm taking pictures today. I need to see them to know it's not me who's nuts here," Alan stated flatly.

I wasn't sure if he was joking. "It reminds me of that movie we watched ages ago, *Gaslight*. You remember? The husband moved things and kept doing weird things with the lights, but told his wife he didn't, trying to drive her insane so he could get her money. Luckily she figured it out in time."

"I'm glad you're here to help me know it's not me. It's not making any sense," Alan said as he walked around, picking up scraps of paper scattered on the floor. "How could we have not known Helen was like this? How could Myron have thought he could take Bruce and not tell you? How in the world are we ever going to be able to leave her? I could go on, but I bet you've been playing the same tapes in your head that I have."

I could only nod. It was all so strange. "Let's get Myron here to pick up everything before she has a chance to do this again tonight. I'll see if I can convince him to come over this afternoon." Alan agreed, and I stepped outside, walking a few houses down to make the call in the one spot I'd been able to find cell reception. Alan went upstairs in case Helen woke up, and I soon joined him.

"He initially balked, but I finally convinced him it was urgent, that if we wait until tomorrow she'll just unpack it all again. He said he could get here around 2 pm. I think we should be gone when he comes; we can leave the side door unlocked. I'm afraid if she sees him it may trigger another round of anger and she's finally starting to calm down. As for the recycling, we'll have to figure out something. I don't want her climbing into the bin every night, and we've got to clean this mess up." I moved into problem-solving mode.

We heard Helen's bedroom door open and her footsteps coming down the narrow hall. She was still in her nightgown with a thin, worn robe hanging over her frail shoulders. It seemed as if she were shrinking more each day. Alan straightened up and walked toward her.

"Good morning, Helen!" his voice bright and friendly. "How was your night? Did you sleep well?" He was clearly going for normalcy.

After breakfast the boxes were brought back into the living room, packed again, as if for the first time, and carried down to the garage. Helen helped as we stacked them neatly for Myron.

Creating a path through the newspapers, Alan suggested maybe they get put in recycling and Helen agreed. "Yes, I don't think the neighbors really want them now," she said, picking several bundles up and walking to the side door. "I also need to get this handle fixed," she said to Alan as she tugged to open it. "I need to call the repairman and get him out here."

"Helen, fixing the door isn't urgent. Let's focus on packing Bruce's stuff and clearing out space down here," his voice reasonable and calm. "If we do one thing at a time, it'll be easier."

"No, I want to get it fixed. I'm going to go call a repairman now." She wasn't in the mood to argue. "This has been bothering me and it needs to get done right now."

"Really, Helen, it can wait. Shelly can call someone tomorrow. For now, help me get these papers into the bin."

"I'll call if I want to. Don't you dare tell me what to do!" She glared at Alan, challenging him to contradict her. He recognized when it was time to stop fighting. Repairing the side door was probably at the bottom of any to-do list, but she was digging in her heels and starting to direct her verbal darts at him. For some reason, she had fixated on it and it was better to let it go.

"Okay, why don't you call," he smiled, hoping to diffuse her hostility. She stomped away as Alan gathered some of the papers and carried them to the bin outside. I followed Helen up the stairs.

When she reached the kitchen I expected her to go straight to the phone, but instead she turned toward the living room. Picking a magazine off the coffee table, she sat down on the sofa and began leafing through it. Not a word was said about the garage door. I certainly wasn't going to bring it up, and when Alan came in a few minutes later, I could see the surprise on his face as well. She'd completely lost the memory of the altercation in the short time it had taken her to move from the garage to the house.

"How about going into San Toro and getting a bite to eat?" I was hungry after all the packing, and knowing Alan, was sure he was starving. It was well past noon and we needed to get out of the house before Myron arrived. "There are a lot of good places on Mission Street; I'm sure we can find something we all agree on." It looked like it'd been awhile since Helen had cooked, and from what I'd seen in the fridge, I figured the stuff in the freezer was equally old. None of us needed food poisoning on top of everything else.

Keeping Helen busy helped her mood, and being out in public kept her from crying. It was a strategy that for the moment was working. She was eager to go out, perhaps a reaction to the many months she'd been trapped in the house after wrecking the car. She made us wait while she found earrings in one of her jewelry boxes and applied lipstick. Always one to have a matching outfit, including shoes and purse, it was intriguing to watch her fussing as she sorted out what to wear. Now that we were spending so much time together it was obvious there was more going on. I wanted to get her into the doctor and figure it out.

As we stood by the counter at the small bistro Alan had selected, Helen looked up at the menu printed on a large sign overhead and peered intently at her choices for a few seconds before turning to me. "What are you going to eat? I can't decide what I want; everything sounds good."

"I think I'll have the fish fillet. Maybe with the sweet potato fries," I said.

"I'll have the same," Helen replied. "I like fish." Once again she chose to eat the same thing as me. She'd never copied me before; was this yet another indication something was off? After Alan decided on the spicy bean and cheese enchiladas, we placed the order, took the proffered plastic number and found a table. Alan filled three glasses of water at the soda fountain and joined us while we waited for our food to arrive.

"Helen, I'm flying back to Seattle tonight; Shelly's going to stay here awhile longer." His tone was conversational. Neither of us knew how she might react. "Maybe the two of you can spend a few days together."

"Oh, that will be nice. I like having company. I wish you were staying as well, but I know work is important and you need to get back." I exhaled softly; a normal reaction to a normal comment; a glimpse of the old Helen. "How long have you been here?" And the moment passed.

Chapter 11

Since my arrival, Helen had complained of sharp pains in her arm 'like it's on fire,' which I seized upon as a reason to take her to the doctor. It didn't matter that it was a neurologist we'd be seeing. A doctor was a doctor, and any excuse to get her in was worth living with a white lie.

"I made an appointment to check out your arm," I mentioned when she came into the dining room. "She can see you this afternoon. Hopefully she'll be able to find out what's going on and help with the pain." With Alan gone, taking his calming influence with him, I didn't want to give her a chance to argue.

The office was small and older than I expected. The doctors in Seattle typically had expensive suites and their fees reflected it, and I had assumed it would be the same in San Toro. The waiting room consisted of a couple of chairs and a table covered with ancient magazines. At least that was familiar. What was it about doctors that they couldn't keep newer periodicals available for their patients? No one was going to catch up on the latest *People* magazine gossip here.

"Mrs. Allaway?" the receptionist asked. "I can take you back now. Would you like your granddaughter to come with you?"

"Yes, please. I'd like her to hear what the doctor says about my arm," Helen replied, not noticing the knowing look on the young woman's face. "I hope she can fix this pain," she continued as we followed her down the hall to a small examining room.

'Thanks for going along with this,' I mouthed silently, catching the receptionist's eye. I'd asked for her help with this duplicity when I'd scheduled the appointment. She smiled like a co-conspirator.

"The doctor will be in shortly." She showed Helen to the table and invited her to sit, then left the room, closing the door behind her.

A soft knock was followed by the sound of the knob turning and a woman entered, tall, fortyish, with a pleasant smile. She extended her hand to Helen, introduced herself as Doctor Campbell, but made no mention of her specialty. "I understand, Mrs. Allaway, that you've been having pain in your arm? Can you describe it to me?" she said as if it were a perfectly reasonable question coming from a neurologist.

As Helen talked, Dr. Campbell lifted her arm, asking questions and examining her carefully. I sat quietly and observed as the doctor slipped in comments and elicited information. It was clear she was conducting a mental status exam under the guise of a physical, and I was impressed with her tact and ability to get information without alerting Helen. After she finished, she invited us to her office where we sat facing her across a cluttered desk.

"There's definitely something going on, Mrs. Allaway, and I believe the problem is coming from your neck. I'd like to send you for an MRI so we can see what's happening." She paused, waiting for that to sink in. "Would it be okay if I sent you to another office for that? I think we can learn a lot and then decide what treatment might help."

"Of course," Helen replied. "I want the pain to stop. It's so upsetting; it shoots up my arm like something's zapping me," she repeated for probably the tenth time.

"Do you make the arrangements or do I need to call?" I asked. "I'm here helping out so I can drive her wherever she needs to go."

Dr. Campbell stood up. "Mrs. Allaway, why don't I take you out front and get you a drink; perhaps you'd like a glass of water? It'll take me a minute to get the information your granddaughter needs for the appointment." As she led Helen down the hall to the waiting room, I heard her speak to the receptionist before she returned, closing the door behind her, and taking a seat.

She clasped her hands in front of her chin, resting her elbows on the desk. "I'd like to get your impressions of Helen. What have you seen going on?" she inquired.

I briefly filled her in on the past few days. It was hard to believe how much had happened only since Friday. "What is it, Dr. Campbell? Is it dementia or something else? How do you diagnose it, anyway?"

"I do think it's a form of dementia," she answered, making no attempt to soften the blow. "I don't know for sure if it is Alzheimer's, which we can't absolutely diagnose until an autopsy is done, but it has most of the hallmarks. How long do you think she's had symptoms?"

"I really can't say, but as I piece it together I imagine several years. Little things, like always asking for my phone number when I'd call, but nothing blatant. It's only been recently that I guess Myron got concerned about his dad, and that's what prompted all of this."

"With couples we often see that one of them holds it together mentally for both of them. They function stronger as a team than they might alone until there's a change in the situation. It sounds like that was happening here: Bruce's brain was working fine; it was his body that was failing. He probably kept them going a lot longer by making sure things got done. Only when she couldn't take care of his physical needs did things fall apart."

In some way it was reassuring that while I hadn't suspected anything, it wasn't simply negligence on my part. Bruce's head and Helen's body had kept them both going and hidden the worst.

"So what are the next steps?"

"The MRI, then a complete psychological exam. That will help establish where she is and isn't struggling. What we learn will determine what kind of support she needs. She clearly doesn't need a locked memory care unit yet; what I don't know is how much help she may need to stay at home. Once we get everything we can talk further." She leaned over and opened a drawer, rustling through a few things before pulling out a card. "Here's the name of the psychologist I work with. He's very good and I think Helen will like him, which is important to get the best results out of her."

She handed me the business card. "My receptionist can set up the MRI for you. I'll also give you a prescription for Helen's neck; it's a stronger anti-inflammatory than the ones you can get over the counter. It's most likely some kind of pinched nerve and those will help until we know more." She scratched out the needed prescription and passed it over. "Do you have any questions? I know this is a lot to take in all at once."

I appreciated her concern. "No, not right now, and yes, it's been a lot. I wasn't expecting this and I haven't really processed it all. I know it's going to hit me one of these days, but in the meantime I'm taking it one step at a time so I don't go nuts. I'm already starting to learn quite a lot just living in the same space as Helen, seeing it up close." I started to gather my things. "Maybe I do have one question: can you recommend any resources for me, perhaps something to read that might help? I'm not really a support group type person."

"I understand. Some people like talking with others going through this, but it's definitely not for everyone. My favorite book for families is *Learning to Speak Alzheimer's*. I don't know if you want to wait for more information first, but I do think that is what we are dealing with, and it'll give you some good ideas how to handle things."

"Thank you." I stood up. "I really appreciate your time."

Alzheimer's. I rolled the word over in my head as I walked back down the hallway. Despite my suspicions, it was still disconcerting to have Dr. Campbell give it that name. I found Helen chatting pleasantly with the receptionist like the old Helen: yakking away and sharing stories. But as I listened more closely I saw the now familiar hints of repetition as she commented on the receptionist's sweater as if seeing it for the first time. She had remarked on it when we first came in, yet it was clear Helen had no memory of that conversation. It was difficult to imagine what must be going on inside her head. Heart failure or cancer I could understand. Someone's brain disintegrating was harder to comprehend. One minute she seemed absolutely normal and 'present,' the next it was as if someone had deleted the moment completely.

An overwhelming sadness enveloped me as I watched for a few seconds before Helen turned and saw me. I pasted on my best smile and walked toward the desk, put an arm around her shoulder, and escorted her out to the car.

Chapter 12

"Once a nurse, always a nurse," Helen cheerfully informed the receptionist at the front desk of the radiology office. "I'm always interested in the new technologies that they didn't have when I was practicing."

"Then I'm sure you'll find the MRI fascinating. Have you ever had one? They're painless; the hardest parts are having to stay still and put up with the noise. But they'll put on music if you'd like." The woman was friendly and engaging, perfect for her role greeting patients who might be experiencing distress. "Brett will be out to get you soon, and he'll explain everything. He'll be happy to answer any questions you have. Have a seat and we'll call your name when he's ready."

We'd barely sat down when a side door pushed opened and a young man called, "Mrs. Allaway?" and smiled as Helen stood up. I heard her chatting away as the door slowly closed and envisioned her talking nonstop throughout the procedure. Fear wouldn't be an issue; getting her to be quiet would. I smiled, remembering Papa Paul's comments about Helen's running commentaries. Just like with me, her chatter had both endeared her to him and annoyed him no end.

I leaned back against the wall, soaking in the quiet. I'd been with Helen five days and the more I was learning, the more I was witnessing, the less sure I was that I'd be leaving any time soon. Since Alan left we'd only been able to talk privately when Helen was ready for bed and I could sneak the phone into the small guest room, shutting the door and whispering as quietly as possible so as not to be overheard. I'd filled him in on our appointment with Dr. Campbell and her suspicions, and told him the schedule for the rest of the week: today the MRI, tomorrow the evaluation with the psychologist, and Friday a meeting alone with an attorney from the list Kim had given me.

Once I was sure Helen was safely ensconced in the MRI room I motioned to the receptionist that I was going to step outside to make a call, in case they needed me.

The sun felt good on my skin. Helen was right, the weather in San Toro was heaven: never too hot and rarely too cold. *Goldilocks*, I laughed to myself as I glanced around to find a place to sit. I spied a low brick wall near the corner of the building where I'd be able to see if they came out looking for me, but was private enough not to disturb any of the surrounding offices. Once I was settled, I pulled out my phone and called Alan, hoping to catch him between meetings.

"Hey," he answered on the second ring. "How'd you know I was sitting here thinking of you, wishing you'd call?"

I wasn't sure if he was telling the truth, but I knew he missed me. I missed him. We weren't often apart, such a contrast from my first marriage where the norm was parallel play: you do your thing and I'll do mine. That's probably why we lasted twenty-plus years; we hardly interacted except over the kids. No fights, but no intensity either; even the divorce had been friendly. I'd envied my grandparents' deep connection, the obvious love they felt for each other, the strong desire to be together. I'd always assumed they'd been extremely lucky until I met Alan.

I took my chances. "How's it going? Just the sugarcoated version; I can't handle the truth right now. I'm sitting in the sun, enjoying the quiet, and I don't need to have it disrupted by stress. So lie to me."

He happily obliged. "Work is wonderful, I love the project I'm on and they're talking raises across the board." Alan chuckled while he spoke. "I'm in line for a promotion and stock prices are through the roof. I can see myself being content here for the next twenty years. How am I doing so far?"

"Perfect. I love it when you talk dirty." I smiled. "Ah, if only it were true. But that's a conversation for another day. In the meantime I choose to remain delusional, it's my new strategy. It's helping me cope here, might as well try it everywhere.

"But shifting to reality, even briefly; the more I learn the more I don't see myself coming home anytime soon. I think you should come back Friday night and stay for the weekend. No matter what happens, I think I need reinforcements to keep going or I may be seeing the doctors as well. I'm not used to nearly constant interaction and nonstop talk. I find myself starting to look for ways to get away, to get some peace and quiet, and be alone with my thoughts. I feel really shitty saying it, because Helen's wonderful. But she's exhausting to take full-time. Thank God Molly's across the street and I can sneak over every now and then for a dose of sanity. I see why Helen likes her so much."

I was grateful for Alan's understanding, knowing he wouldn't judge my reactions. We both clearly cared about Helen. "Why don't you book the flight and I'll take care of everything else. I'll ask the neighbors to watch the cats and pick up the mail. Schedule me to fly home early Monday; I don't have any meetings until after lunch. We can always change things if it needs to be longer."

"Sounds like a plan. I'll email you a list of things to bring for me. I'm getting sick of the few clothes I have, plus I'd like my running shoes and iPod along with the rest of my workout stuff. I've got to get out, if only to clear my head, and I think running will be okay with Helen. She shows me she can still do her Air Force exercises: push-ups, squats... old school stuff. She cracks me up; she's been doing them as long as I can remember and takes great pride in her fitness."

"As long as you're really specific I think I can find what you want. But I mean details, details, details! If not, you're stuck with whatever I pick out, and you know how good I am at that without you here." I could hear him smiling. Alan hated packing for himself, let alone searching through my closet for pants or shirts he wouldn't know from Adam. But he also wanted to help and this was something he could do.

We chatted a few more minutes before saying goodbye. He had to attend another of his endless meetings and I wanted to get back inside to be there when Helen finished. I felt a mixture of emotions as I placed the phone back into my purse and slid off the wall. Relief Alan would soon be back, frustration that it wouldn't be for several days, and concern for Helen.

Once inside I pulled out my Kindle and spent the rest of the hour catching up on reading for book club. I wanted to finish this month's selection, but hadn't had as much time for it as I'd hoped, though we typically spent far more time talking, laughing, and drinking wine than discussing the books. It had been one of the first places where I'd felt part of the neighborhood after we'd married and moved to our new home. I was clearly the old lady of the group as most still had kids in school, but friendships developed that went beyond the monthly meetings. We hiked, celebrated birthdays, and ran half-marathons together, and were there for each other through tough times. I hoped I'd be back before the next gathering; I could use their support.

I heard the door open and saw Helen emerge, as chatty as she'd been when she'd gone in. Brett smiled and nodded as he escorted her over to me. I stood as they approached.

"She was a perfect patient," he reported. Helen beamed. "I was able to get some really good impressions and the radiologist will share them with Dr. Campbell as soon as he has a chance to review them. Do we have your contact number in case we have any questions?" He glanced at the chart. I'd given them my cell number and had explained the situation to the receptionist when Helen was out of earshot. "Ah, I see it here, we're all good." He must have noticed the instructions.

Helen turned to Brett, slightly concerned. "I'm sure I fell asleep and it might affect the results. I hope it didn't ruin anything."

"No, as I said while you were in there, it's fine if you sleep. You don't need to be awake for it at all," he replied reassuringly. "Anyway, we'll call Dr. Campbell with the results and I'm sure she'll be in touch." Closing the folder, he bid her goodbye one more time and went back inside.

On the ride home Helen continued to obsess about falling asleep. No amount of logic was going to dissuade her from the worry, and after a few attempts, I simply gave up. Arguing with her had never been easy, and now it was impossible. I hoped the psychologist would be able to offer some insights tomorrow.

Chapter 13

It was surprisingly easy to get Helen to agree to the appointments I had scheduled. She was still convinced they all centered on the pain in her arm, which thankfully, was beginning to subside with the anti-inflammatories Dr. Campbell had prescribed. An MRI made sense, but how could I explain a psychological evaluation? It would be a far more detailed mental status exam; how might I link it to her neck and arm?

Luckily she seemed to enjoy getting out of the house and all the attention she was receiving, and didn't question anything when we parked in front of an older building on the outskirts of downtown. We climbed the outside wooden stairs to the second floor and entered another dated, cramped waiting room. San Toro was very well-to-do, but so many of the buildings were ancient, and not particularly intriguing architecturally. Was that part of its charm? Whatever the reason, the choices for seating were either the sagging couch along the wall or the metal chair in the corner.

After checking in with the receptionist behind the sliding glass window, I opted for support and settled onto the chair. Helen wandered around the tiny room, commenting on the décor and reading the bulletin board hanging on the wall by the entrance. Other than the receptionist, we were alone. I murmured an 'um' or 'ah' every now and then to show I was listening to her chatter, happy she was occupied with the mundane and not questioning why we were here.

After a short wait the door opened and a middle-aged man neatly dressed in tan Dockers and a light blue button-down shirt came over to Helen. "Hi, I'm Dr. Scott," he said as he extended his hand. "You must be Mrs. Allaway."

"Oh, please, call me Helen. Mrs. Allaway is too formal." She took his hand and smiled up at him. "Nice to meet you as well. I hope you can help with my arm, although I'm not really sure what you'll do."

Once again I'd had a brief conversation with the office when setting up the appointment.

Dr. Scott responded to Helen. "Yes, well, let's see what we can learn. We'll do a few paper and pencil tests for an hour or so, and then we'll take a short rest. After that you'll come back in and we'll just chat. Will that be okay?" She nodded. 'Then come on in with me and we'll get started." He opened the door and led her inside. I settled in for another long wait.

When she returned, she was annoyed but thankfully, not angry. "It was silly. He had me draw circles and count numbers. I don't understand what this has to do with my arm. He's very nice, but why did he need me to do that baby stuff? I'm not an idiot; those tests were simple!" She looked tired, and I suspected the tests were more challenging than she let on.

"Let's go get a cup of hot chocolate and a muffin at the coffee stand across the street. It'll refresh you before you go back in." Distraction still worked, and I knew the short walk outside would be good for her mood and her energy. "I'd love a chai tea."

Returning to the office thirty minutes later, Dr. Scott was ready for phase two of the testing. It sounded like this would be a conversational exam and perhaps more enjoyable for Helen than performing tasks that demanded skills she may no longer possess. Being reminded of her deficiencies couldn't feel good, and besides, she loved to talk, no matter the subject.

I took advantage of the break to step outside and call my mom. I needed to update her on Helen's situation. I hadn't phoned since that first night in Seattle and knew I had delayed long enough.

This time I got lucky. The robotic, disembodied voice of her answering machine greeting informed me 'no one is home; please leave a message,' which I did. A brief overview of Helen's status would suffice to alleviate any guilt. Glad to be done with that chore, I went back inside to wait.

Another hour passed before they appeared in the doorway, conversing pleasantly. *Thank goodness, it looks like it went well.* I didn't want our evening to be spent complaining about her visit.

"We'll chat more at our next appointment," Dr. Scott said. "It's been a delight spending time with you today." He smiled and said goodbye before closing the door behind him.

"All done?" I inquired. "Ready to get some food? I'm starving, and I bet you are, too." We spent the rest of the afternoon downtown, lunching at a tiny Mexican restaurant and popping in and out of shops. She kept commenting on the latest fashions that teens were wearing, wondering how the boys found saggy pants comfortable or the girls thought baring bellies was ladylike. I had to agree about the baggy jeans. We shared a scoop of ice cream at the boutique creamery before heading home. We rounded out the evening with leftovers for dinner, and watching one of Helen's favorite news shows before heading to bed. No drama. A sigh of relief.

Chapter 14

By midweek we'd established a routine. I had to find some consistency for my own sake, if not for Helen's. The crying spells had lessened considerably, but she demanded a lot of attention and focus. She would obsess over some small detail, fussing and becoming agitated, and then her mood would quickly change as her eye caught something else. I was exhausted simply witnessing it. I wondered what it must be like for Helen; did it wear her down or was it possible her forgetfulness and scattered attention was actually a blessing?

Sharing breakfast, cleaning up, going for a walk through the neighborhood, and driving into San Toro for doctor appointments and lunch filled much of our time. On a couple of occasions we stopped in front of Molly's to chat with her while the twins played in the yard. Helen lit up when she saw them, her love of children apparent as she watched them in a game of tag or playing ball. The kids enjoyed competing for the adults' attention. Even I found satisfaction in such simple pleasures, momentarily forgetting the nightmare we were living the rest of the day.

Late afternoons were spent looking through old photo albums. My grandparents had travelled extensively, visiting many of the people Papa Paul had met in his work with international subsidiaries, and after each trip they compiled a book filled with pictures and narrative. The shelf in the office closet was crammed with notebooks labeled with the country and year of their visit. Pulling them down one at a time, Helen told stories of their travels, providing welcome entertainment. It was surprising, given her struggles with day-to-day routines, that she could so easily recall details of meals they'd eaten or tours they'd taken years before simply by looking at a photo.

"I remember you and Papa Paul talking about your trips. I always wanted you to take me with you, but you never did. Of course, now that I'm an adult I can certainly understand why you didn't want a pesky kid tagging along!" I laughed. We were sitting side by side on the couch, paging through one of the heavy books Helen had chosen. "I know it was partly because I wanted to escape from home, but it was also because I'd inherited Papa Paul's passion for adventure."

"When he travelled for work he loved meeting people and hearing their stories. After he retired we planned many of our trips around visiting them, and then as he got older we started going on cruises. The ships made it easier for him to get around without having to move from hotel to hotel," Helen reminisced. "Did you know he only gave up international travel because it hurt to sit so long on airplanes? He was ninety! He never did quit wanting to go places."

"I do know that. As long as he could drive somewhere he could continue exploring. You even came to Seattle to celebrate his ninety-second birthday," I reminded her. During moments like this it was easy to forget Helen's dementia; it felt like the conversations we'd had during our earlier visits.

I thought back on all the times we'd sat in Papa Paul's room, particularly after I'd finished high school and began coming to San Toro on my own. Without others around we were able to have deeper conversations, not only about travel but also about life. I turned to them for advice before pursuing graduate studies; I could talk honestly about the conflicted relationship with my mom, or ask their viewpoints about the different guys I dated. I appreciated their questions, the way they'd gently force me to look at things from multiple perspectives. I knew they supported me, not just because I was their granddaughter, but because they were interested in me as a person. I felt myself tearing up as I realized that the Helen I had relied on, the person who had helped guide me over the years, was now only available in fragmented pieces.

Whenever I could sneak away I spent time on the computer. With all the uncertainty going on, I juggled clients as best as I could, but just as often I surfed Facebook or the Internet hoping to get a few moments of connection to the world back home. It had helped when Alan was still around, but once he was gone I couldn't get needed quiet with Helen's constant fussiness and desire for conversation. I was eager for Alan to bring my gear; getting out for runs would offer a much-needed escape. Walking with Helen didn't offer the same workout that running did, mentally or physically, and I needed both.

I still had one obstacle left to figure out: how to get away alone for the appointment with the attorney. I didn't want Helen to know what I was doing, and certainly didn't want her to come along. *Work. I'll tell Helen I have to take care of some client work. In her current state I think I can get away with it without too much trouble.*

After sharing a pleasant cup of tea and light conversation over breakfast I broached the subject. "I have to go into San Toro for a few hours; I won't be gone long," I casually informed Helen. "I have some client issues I need to tend to."

"Fine. Go. You just do what you need to do." Her voice was hard as she stood up abruptly, carrying her cup into the kitchen. "You've always been like that. Very cold and analytical, I don't need you here." I was stunned. What had I done? How had her mood flipped so suddenly?

"Helen, what are you talking about? I'm not analyzing anything! Why are you saying that?" I didn't know what to do: reassure or defend? The accusation was so outrageous and uncharacteristic of our relationship.

"Oh, you've always analyzed things. I know you; you've always done that. Watching people, looking at them through your therapist eyes." She wasn't backing down as she turned to glare at me. "Leave. I don't care what you do." She spun back around to the sink, turning on the faucet and making it clear she had nothing further to say.

Still in shock, I walked out of the kitchen. I needed to shower before the appointment, and maybe we both just needed some time apart. My mind raced as I picked out clothes for the day and went back down the hall toward the bathroom. I paused before closing the door. I could hear Helen clanking things around in the kitchen, and felt the urge to go back and try to clear the air. But the instinct to stay away was stronger, whether it was the smart move or simply avoidance really didn't matter; I couldn't handle another dose of Helen's venom.

Turning on the water, I adjusted the temperature before dropping my pajamas on the small bench Helen kept in the bathroom and stepped into the old yellow tub. The flow from the showerhead felt good, and I stood under it for several seconds, trying to calm my emotions. Tears mingled with the stream pouring over my face, and before I realized it, I was sobbing.

Papa Paul, help me! Help Helen be okay. Help her accept whatever it is that is going on. Help her find peace! I felt so alone and overwhelmed with everything. Why was I being attacked like this? *Please help us both!* I offered it as prayer, a plea to the man we both had adored. I prided myself on being able to handle things, to be responsible and to figure everything out, but as my tears began to subside I admitted it was all too much. As my breathing slowed and my mind quieted, I pondered what I had done to elicit Helen's rage, and what I could do to get things back to normal.

She's not reacting to your words, she reacting to your stress. The thoughts came unexpectedly. *The calmer you can stay the better it is for her. You have to stay calm.* It made sense. My body language had most definitely conveyed my stress trying to figure out a way to escape the house. Because the reality was I did want to escape. I knew what was expected of me, and I wanted to be the good granddaughter, yet those expectations were suffocating me. Secretly I liked the idea of being a saint, of everyone saying how wonderful I was for stepping in and taking care of Helen. I hated to admit it but I felt a sense of pride in being so capable and willing to drop everything for my family. But now that I was actually living with Helen, even temporarily, I discovered I wasn't enjoying the reality of it.

I felt trapped. In many ways I was; who else would step in and take care of her? No one else was around, and certainly no one Helen trusted. But was I really trapped? I had freely chosen the role many years earlier, sitting in on all the meetings with the attorney, having numerous discussions with Papa Paul before he died, and many more with Helen after he passed. I knew what they both wanted, I knew what I had freely agreed to, and I couldn't imagine doing anything else. She was my only living grandmother, the one I'd been closest to, and there was no way I'd abandon her. The situation sucked, but I wasn't staying there out of obligation. I loved Helen, and I cared deeply about what happened to her. I just had to figure out a better way to take care of both of us so we didn't kill each other in the process.

Chapter 15

When I emerged from the bathroom I found Helen sitting in the living room, reading the paper and sipping a cup of tea. Cautiously, I approached her.

"Hey, Helen. What's going on in the news today?" I hoped the neutral topic would elicit a positive response. "Anything exciting?"

"The usual. This paper is mostly local happenings, not much of interest for you. I stopped getting the national paper a while ago. Too much to read so I just watch the TV news instead." She spoke as if nothing had happened only thirty minutes earlier. "You look nice. What are you all dressed up for?"

Here it comes. She clearly didn't recall our previous conversation or her sharp rebuke. "I have some work I need to take care of in San Toro this morning. Will you be okay here while I'm gone?" I tried to keep my tone and body light and calm, hoping it would keep her equally calm. "I should only be a couple of hours. We can get something to eat when I get back."

"Of course I'll be fine. You go and do what you need to. I'll do some chores and maybe take a shower myself. Don't worry about me." The change in tone was dramatic. "Take your time."

"Sure, I should be back by noon or so." I bent over to give her a kiss on the cheek. "Let's go to that new organic place on Elm Street. It looked good when we walked by yesterday." I guessed Helen wouldn't remember that suggestion when I returned, but that didn't matter. What did matter was I felt relaxed and Helen was responding positively. "See you soon; love you!" I called out as I shut the front door. Leaning against it for a second, I let out a long breath. *Thank you, Papa Paul.*

The attorney's office was easy to locate, but street parking, always a challenge, was unusually difficult in the small main section of town today. After circling the block twice I pulled into the parking garage a few streets down and walked. I'd deliberately left the house early to get some time alone. I'd had so little of it over the past week, and most of that had been hiding in the guest room pretending to be asleep or hunkered over the computer, pretending to work.

I spied a Peet's coffee shop on the corner and the thought of a chai tea was enticing. Ordering it to go, I read some of the flyers on the bulletin board advertising upcoming plays, talks, and community events while I waited. Then, warm cup in hand, I walked the remainder of the way toward the newer two-story brick building that housed the lawyer I'd chosen.

I scanned the lobby as I entered. It was tastefully decorated, but not ostentatious. The receptionist smiled and welcomed me by name, and seeing the cup in my hand said, "Normally I'd offer you coffee or tea, but you look like you already have some. Do you need a refill?" I shook my head no.

"James will be out in a minute. If you'd like to take a seat, I'll let him know you're here."

I found a chair and settled my cup on the small side table, picking up a *People* magazine off the pile to glance through while I waited. *At least this place has current issues. Hopefully that bodes well for his expertise as well.* Soon a pleasant-looking man appeared, early fifties, wearing a light gray sport coat over an unbuttoned shirt collar. *Professional but not too formal,* I liked that.

"You must be Shelly," he said, extending his hand. "I'm James Montgomery. Very nice to meet you. Let's go to the conference room so we can talk." He led the way down the hall and stopped in front of an open door. Stepping aside to let me in, he invited me to sit at the small rectangular table in the middle of the room before taking the chair across from me.

"I understand you're here to talk about your mother?' he glanced at the opened folder in front of him. "Is that correct?"

"Actually, it's my step-grandmother. She was with Paul, my grandfather, from the time I was born, so I've always viewed her simply as my grandmother." I paused. "I'm here because it looks like she suffers from some kind of dementia and I need to know what to do. I'm the only family member she counts on, and I'm also the one who'll be in charge if anything happens. I have a copy of her Trust, which I brought with me. I wanted to talk to you before I bring her in to give you some background."

"Let's take a look," he said, as I pushed the thick packet across the table. "But before I do, tell me what's been happening. What do you know about the Trust and what's your role? How about we start there." He pulled a yellow legal pad in front of him, ready to take notes.

"My grandparents created the Trust years before my grandfather passed. He was twenty-three years older and assumed he'd die first, and he wanted to make sure she was taken care of. He adored her; she was everything to him.

"When he died, I went to the attorney with her. I think she chose me to handle things because I was closest to her and maybe the most like my grandfather: level-headed and responsible with money.

"The Trust is pretty straightforward. Helen lives off of it and has control of it until she dies, then my mother gets the interest and income from it, but can't touch the principal. When she dies the Trust ends and whatever is left in it is distributed to my brother and me."

I stopped to finish the last sip of my chai, savoring the taste despite its now cooled temperature. I got up and walked over to the trash receptacle and tossed the empty cup inside before returning to my seat and facing James. "My mother is a disaster with money, so they didn't want her to blow it all, and they had a pretty conflicted relationship with my brother over the years. He was the rebellious one who got into drugs, and although he cleaned up years ago he can still be argumentative. I guess I was the quiet kid, the good student, didn't make waves; thus, I'm assuming, the reason they put me in charge. What else would you like to know?"

He'd been taking notes and skimming the paperwork I'd brought while I spoke, and now he sat back in his chair, lightly tapping his pen on the pad for a moment before speaking.

"What you have is called a generation-skipping Trust. From what I hear and see, it was established years ago that you would be the Successor Trustee and Power of Attorney for the Trust in the event Helen either died or became incapacitated. That appears to be clear in the paperwork and makes things a lot easier. Has anyone said she is mentally incapable of making decisions?" I appreciated his calm demeanor and focus on facts.

"Well, this is why I've come to town. Bruce, her partner of the past eleven years, was recently moved to a skilled nursing facility because she's not able to care for him anymore, and there's a concern she isn't able to care for herself consistently, either. Dr.

Campbell, her neurologist, said that while it is likely she has Alzheimer's, she is still very much aware; the diagnosis alone doesn't mean incapacity. From what I can gather her mind is still fine in many areas, it's just the day-to-day, short-term stuff that's really messed up. She can talk intelligently about the news she's watching or reading in the paper; we can have conversations about family, neighbors, or stories from the past. But she'll go into her bedroom to put on jewelry and forget why she was there, or struggle to understand a menu to decide what to eat. She's been through quite a shock with Bruce's departure and it's hard to tell how that has affected her, apart from whatever else is going on. I'll know more when I meet with the psychologist again on Tuesday to hear the results of his testing." I tried to be as honest as possible in my assessment.

"Okay, once we know what he says then we will have a better idea which actions to take. It's going to be important to have you named as Co-Trustee and added to all her banking and investment accounts. According to these documents, it's what she intended anyway so we aren't changing anything. If the doctors believe she's capable of making these decisions it's a lot easier than going to court and having you made conservator. If they say she's already too far gone, then we'll have to go the legal route. She has to be aware enough to be deemed able to sign documents," he paused. "Do you think she is?"

"I'm not an expert, but I think so. After the doctor's visit I'll bring her here and you can meet her, and if she's capable, she can sign papers." It felt better to have doctors making the determination, not me.

"Sounds reasonable. In the meantime, let's go over a few details. First off, I notice you refer to your grandmother as Helen. Is that what you call her?"

"Yes. I'm not really sure why we never called her grandma or some other endearing name; we've just always referred to her as Helen. I'm guessing it was because she was so close in age to my mom when she came into my grandfather's life and it was hard for Ann to see her in that role, or maybe it was my mother's way of defining her as an outsider. I've never really thought about it," I answered.

"Remarriages and family dynamics always bring complications. It's one of the things I deal with a lot specializing in estates and trusts. I wish I could say it brings out the best in people, but sadly, it's rarely the case. Although my perception is most likely skewed, since clients don't need much assistance when it's going smoothly." He paused to glance at the paperwork in front of him before resuming. "I assume there aren't any name changes from these documents; if there are, bring them with you. Your name is listed as Shelly. Is that short for Michelle?"

"No, that's my full name. My mother loved the theatre and Shelley Winters was one of her favorite actresses. My brother was named after Gary Cooper. I suppose it could have been worse; she idolized Ethel Merman. Thank God she didn't pass that one on to me!"

"Um, yeah, you did get lucky there. Not exactly a fashionable name these days," James smiled. "Okay. Let's schedule a meeting for the three of us early next week. Call me beforehand with a synopsis of the test results, and I'll make a determination based on what I see in conjunction with his assessment. It's a pretty defined line what will constitute consent or not." He picked up the Trust. "Do you mind if I have my assistant make a copy?" I nodded.

He stepped out of the room for a minute, then returned with the original Trust, which he handed to me and a copy, which he laid on top of his legal pad of notes.

The conference over, he walked me back down the hall. "I look forward to meeting her. It'll help me understand the situation a little better." We shook hands and then he turned to the receptionist. "Can you please schedule Ms. Johnson for an appointment Wednesday?"

One more item checked off my list, I left the office and walked the few blocks back to the car. I glanced at my watch: 11:15, plenty of time to get back to the house, pick Helen up, and head out for lunch. I pulled out my cell phone, pushing the number for Alan. Filling him in on the morning's meeting, I asked him about his day.

"It's all fine. I'm packed to go straight to the airport after my last meeting. I'll be leaving here around four." I wondered if it really was fine or if he was simply minimizing his frustrations for my benefit. Did I really want to know how he felt about work? Honestly, at the moment, no. For once I appreciated his protectiveness.

"Okay, see you tonight. I suggest you eat dinner before you get here. We still aren't cooking so you'd be left to scavenge the cereal supply and I doubt that'd be enough food for you." I wanted to keep it light as well. "I love you, thank you for coming back. I can certainly use your support. Besides, I miss you." There was plenty of time for heavy discussions later.

Chapter 16

The weekend offered the first real break I'd experienced since listening to Molly's phone message just over a week ago. Had it really only been that long? Although Helen's crying and anger outbursts had lessened considerably, Alan's calm presence was still a welcome respite. His ability to sit quietly with her, listening to her stories with genuine caring despite her numerous tangents and now obvious repetitions, was admirable. I'd witnessed his patience with his mother after she'd had an aneurism, sitting by her bedside softly stroking her cheek and talking in whispers to her. I'd felt it when confronted with my mother's incessant demands for financial assistance, as we navigated the fine line between caring and resentment and found solutions. I knew I offered the same in return, a safe place to talk about the stresses with his first wife that never seemed to end or his dissatisfaction with his current work situation. We trusted each other and were good together. I was grateful for his willingness to set everything else aside to be with me, to be here with Helen.

Before we met with the psychologist I'd managed to clear out most of the food in the freezer, sneaking it into the outside trash while Helen was otherwise occupied. It felt funny to be sorting through her belongings, but by now I knew that out of sight really did mean out of mind in her present-day world. Move something that had been in place for years and she'd catch it immediately, but change anything new and it was forgotten within minutes. Having Bruce's things packed and gone certainly helped. Helen still talked about him constantly, but the sight of some small trinket no longer triggered her rage by reminding her of his callous abandonment. With no further doctor's appointments on the calendar for the next two days we were free to spend the weekend relaxing.

On Saturday, I suggested driving over the hills to the beach, stopping for lunch in one of the quaint coastal towns that dotted the shore. Helen loved playing tour guide, pointing out places she'd visited with Papa Paul or Bruce, giving the history of local landmarks, and generally acting like the Helen of old. Growing up, I wanted her to stop trying to educate me about the building Frank Lloyd Wright had designed or the reasons she and Papa Paul had stopped going to the neighborhood church. Such details were boring to me as teenager who only wanted to be home with friends. Now I welcomed the normalcy of it, and even appreciated many of her stories. I had to admit that as I got older, many of the things that had once numbed me to sleep I now found fascinating.

We stayed closer to home Sunday, wandering in and out of shops in the artsy town just south of San Toro. Helen was intrigued by one jewelry store in particular, commenting on the unique designs. I saw several things I liked as well, and was pleasantly surprised when Alan presented me with a pair of earrings during lunch as we sat on the deck of a small seafood restaurant, watching the sailboats in the bay. His thoughtfulness touched me and his well-timed gesture once again averted an emotional meltdown as Helen teared up reminiscing about the last time Bruce had taken her on his boat.

On the way home we stopped at the local video store to rent a movie for later that evening. No sad movies, no reminders of good times with Bruce; we settled on *Mamma Mia!* the light musical based on ABBA songs, a couple of which Helen recognized. Prompted by certain scenes in the movie, she interjected some of her travel stories, remembering visiting Greece with Papa Paul, but mostly she just enjoyed watching the actors as they sang and danced across the small TV screen in her living room. By ten p.m. she had nodded off in her chair, soft snores escaping with every few breaths. I watched her for several minutes.

"This reminds me of peeking in on the kids when they were small. Such whirlwinds of energy during the day, and so peaceful when they finally passed out," I whispered to Alan sitting next to me on the sofa under the window. "It's nice to see her so calm, no anxieties, no worries. I think she had fun this weekend, and I think it's been a long time since she has. I wish it could last."

Alan put his arm around me and brought me close. It felt good to be held and for a few minutes we sat silently, watching Helen, before it was time to gently nudge her awake and walk her down the hall to her bedroom.

Chapter 17

"Welcome back, Helen," Dr. Scott greeted us as he opened the door and invited us into his office. He remembered her preference for using her first name. "Would you like something to drink before we get started?" He waved his hand at the side table filled with a large coffee pot, mismatched mugs, and assorted creamers and sugars. Alan had flown home yesterday and I was once again alone with Helen. We had spent the day peacefully with no appointments and no errands to run other than our usual lunch excursion, and I enjoyed the change of pace. But now I was looking forward to creating an action plan. I couldn't stay in San Toro indefinitely, and I couldn't leave Helen in her current state.

"Yes, a coffee with one sweetener would be lovely," Helen replied. "Do you want something, Shelly?" she turned to me, always the hostess.

"Sure, same, but with creamer would be great," I offered, hoping to keep things easy and comfortable. I had no idea how Helen would respond to her mental status being discussed and Dr. Scott's recommendations. We'd given her the option to meet with him alone, but she had insisted that I accompany her. I was relieved to have the chance to gauge Helen's reactions first hand in Dr. Scott's presence.

As we stepped into the crowded office, I looked around and compared it to my neat, expansive space. There were the typical office-style upholstered chairs separated by a small table underneath one of the windows. A large rectangular table was pushed up against the second window, overlooking the back of the building. Unlike all the other surfaces, it was clutter free, presumably where patients could concentrate on tasks presented to them when they were tested. One wall was covered with shelves floor to ceiling, filled with books, many of which I recognized from my own years of graduate studies. Dr. Scott's desk was stacked with papers and folders, and as Helen and I settled into the chairs clearly meant for patients, the doctor pulled out one of the files before turning his massive swivel chair in our direction and sitting down.

"Helen, first, I want to say you did a great job last week on all these tests. You're a very well-rounded and intelligent woman who has seen much in your life," he smiled at her as he opened the file. "You've had a wonderful career as a nurse, travelled the world, and been active in many important guilds and groups since your retirement. You make me feel lazy by comparison!" I glanced at Helen. I knew she responded well to males, and the flattery was having the desired effect: she was beaming. A smart man to get off on the right foot; I was curious to see how he'd handle the hard parts.

"We looked at many things the other day, such as what you remember from long ago, and what you are able to remember right after I presented something to you — short term," he started. Helen nodded as he spoke. "You did very well with long-term memory questions. You have great recall of events of the past and knowledge you've acquired over time. You understand what's going on in the world and have well-formed opinions about many things. I enjoyed our chat about the World Affairs Council and the symphony." He paused, shuffling the papers in front of him, pulling one out and turning it for us to see.

"Here are some of the results from that portion of our interview. You can see my notes and the scale here. You did very well." I peeked sideways at Helen. She was still smiling. Thankfully, she didn't question what any of this had to do with her arm.

"What I also noticed," he continued, pulling out another paper from the file, "was that it was hard for you to remember things that were new, things that I asked you to repeat after hearing them or seeing them once. For example, here's one where I had you repeat a series of numbers one minute after I showed them to you." He turned the paper for Helen to see. She glanced at it briefly and waved her hand.

"Oh, that's because they were silly questions. I can't be bothered to remember numbers like that. Who can?" Another of her dismissive comments, her defense against her failing memory. *I'm too tired, I'm too old, and it's silly*; the excuses varied but the point was the same. She couldn't remember and she was embarrassed to admit it.

"Yes, they're silly questions; you're correct." Dr. Scott replied kindly, helping Helen maintain her sense of dignity. He turned toward the computer behind him, moving the mouse as he did, bringing the screen back to life. "But what concerns me with some of these tests is that I think it's hard for you to remember things day to day, things you need to be able to take care of yourself, like cooking your meals. As I understand it, that's part of the reason Bruce had to move out." He looked at me for confirmation. I nodded. Then he moved on before Helen had a chance to protest.

"I also want to show you the results of your MRI. Dr. Campbell and I agreed it made sense for me to go over them with you both since you were coming in today. If you come over here I can share what we learned from them."

Helen was fascinated by science, and the chance to see her brain was intriguing. We got out of our chairs and huddled around Dr. Scott's screen.

"If you look here, there are spaces, these white areas, where we wouldn't expect to see any. The overall size of the brain is smaller than it should be, as if it's shrunken. These images, combined with all the other test results, indicate Alzheimer's, although, as you know, we can't diagnose for certain at this time."

I watched Helen listen to Dr. Scott's words. It was as if she were hearing about a stranger, not herself. Her face was filled with curiosity, questions forming as she looked at the images in front of her.

"How can you tell what this line here means?" she queried. "How are they able to measure the size and know if it's shrunk?" She listened intently as he pointed things out on the screen, and for the next few minutes Helen the nurse was in control of the conversation.

Seemingly satisfied with his answers, she sat back down in her chair. I followed her, waiting to see where the discussion would go next.

"So what does all that mean?" Helen asked. "I don't have Alzheimer's, so this is a pointless conversation." She looked at Dr. Scott as if defying him to contradict her.

"Helen, I know this is hard to hear, and harder to accept. But the tests, and my interview with you, confirm my conclusions that you're having problems with your memory, especially your short-term memory. As I said, I can't diagnose Alzheimer's definitively, but based on all the evidence I would say yes, you have it." He paused for his words to sink in.

"Well, I'm just getting old and I'm tired, that's why I forget things. There's nothing wrong with me other than that. Of course, I've been under stress, taking care of Bruce these last few years." I wanted to interrupt, having heard these excuses for days now. While Helen fervently believed what she was saying, it wasted time repeating herself again and again. But I remained silent, letting the psychologist direct the conversation.

"One of the characteristics many with the disease have is not recognizing the symptoms in themselves," he interrupted. "It's such a strange thing, and I understand your confusion." As always, his bearing was kind, softening the harshness of the diagnosis.

"You're still very capable of understanding big things and making major decisions, but you're forgetful about the smaller details," he went on. "That creates a concern for your well-being. Once your granddaughter goes back to Seattle, you'll be alone. You're not able to drive. As long as Bruce was with you, someone was around if something went wrong, but now you're isolated. With him gone it's not safe for you to be in the house by yourself." His voice was calm, reassuring. He'd obviously had this conversation with many other patients and was prepared for Helen's blowback.

"How dare you say that I can't take care of myself? I've taken care of myself all my life! So what if I forget a few things, that doesn't mean I'm an idiot!" Her voice was curt and clipped. "What exactly are you saying?"

"What I'm saying is you need to have someone come and live with you, or if that isn't possible, you'll need to move into a place where you can be cared for safely." He paused to watch her reaction. She glared at him. "It's my professional opinion that it would be dangerous for you to continue living on your own." He waited to see how she was going to take this.

"That is ridiculous. I don't need a babysitter, and there's no way

I'm leaving my home. You can't force me to go!" She sat back against her seat, satisfied that she had made her point.

I watched quietly without comment. I had spoken with Dr. Scott on the phone before the appointment, so his information came as no surprise. We'd strategized how to get Helen to accept his recommendations, knowing she would not acquiesce easily, if at all. He'd warned me that it's common for patients at her stage of the disease to be unable to comprehend they have Alzheimer's and that using logic to explain what was needed wouldn't work. She wouldn't see the problem that was so obvious to everyone else, and there was no point in trying to prove it to her.

"Helen, I know it's hard to accept. But I have an obligation to make sure you're safe. It's my opinion, based on all that I've seen, that you have to have supervision. If Shelly were nearby it might be different. But you were very clear that you would never want to live in Seattle, and she can't move down here. Therefore, you have to agree to either have someone come to live with you or find a place to go."

"And what if I say no?" she countered. "What if I refuse?"

"Then I have no choice but to contact the local authorities and let them know. I'm obligated to tell them if I believe you are a danger to yourself, and I believe you are if you live alone." He introduced the plan we had concocted. It was probably stretching the truth, but I figured it was the only way to get her to agree to a move. I already knew she'd never let someone move in, and even if she did, they'd drive each other crazy. Helen was too entrenched in her role as caregiver to ever let someone take care of her, and she'd resent the intrusion into her space.

"What? That's absurd!" Helen shouted. "How dare you!"

Dr. Scott remained calm, letting her vent; this must be difficult for him. It was torturous for me to watch her pain, anger, and confusion. Neither of us wanted to take away her freedom, but her dementia, whether Alzheimer's or something else, was giving us no choice. It was now obvious to me that she was a danger to herself. What if she turned on the stove and went to bed, forgetting she'd done so, and the kitchen caught fire? What if she couldn't remember to eat? I'd already witnessed a sufficient number of incidents to cause concern. What would happen with no one in the house as things got worse?

I'd been reading the book Dr. Campbell recommended and learned that the sooner we moved Helen, the better to take advantage of her current ability to still form memories and attachments to caregivers. The longer we waited the worse it would be. For now she could understand why she was moving. Later it would only terrify her to be in a strange place, with strange people, and no comprehension as to why she was there.

He waited several minutes for her to calm down. "It's better if you decide where to go rather than have the state send in a social worker. If that happens they'll make the decision for you. That would be far worse, wouldn't it? This way you have control over where to go; you and Shelly can visit places and see what you like. There really are nice places to choose from, lots of active people, good care." Creating a paradox, where the best choice was for her to feel in control rather than giving it to the state, was our strategy. I knew, faced with those choices, which one Helen would pick. And once she did, she could claim it was her decision.

Helen and Dr. Scott went back and forth a few more times, but she was wearing down. His demeanor, combined with her respect for male doctors, won out in the end. She liked him, and that helped. As we stood to leave she even gave him a hug, her animosity momentarily forgotten. I was relieved: one obstacle down, a hundred more to go.

Chapter 18

"I thought it went well while we were in his office," I related the experience to Alan. "Although she fought him at first, she finally agreed that we find her a place to live. I think he scared her with his talk of the state making the decision for her. I felt bad, using that as a threat, but so far everyone is fully onboard that she can't stay here alone."

I'd smuggled Helen's portable phone into the tiny guestroom that had become my refuge. She'd finally gone to bed a half-hour earlier; it was the first chance I had to connect with Alan without the risk of being overheard.

"But then she started in all over again on the way home. 'I don't care what he says. I don't have to leave my house! Who does he think he is telling me I need a babysitter! I'm perfectly capable of taking care of myself.' You get the idea; you've seen her," I continued. "I can't tell you how many times I had to repeat her dilemma: either she picks or the state picks. Thank goodness the doctor suggested that as a way to deflect it from any of us; she can re-direct her anger at the rules and still see him as an ally. She really did like him."

"So what does that mean for us? It's sounding more and more like you'll need to be there for a while if you have to find a place for her." His voice was calm and reasonable. It always helped to talk to him, to bring the conversation to the practical. "And what's going to happen with the house? You're probably going to need me there for more than a weekend."

"Yeah. Once we can get her to agree to move, I'll need to find someone to help us decide what to do with the house. I don't think it's a great time for selling; plus it may be too much for her to deal with now. At least she owns the place outright.

"Come Friday, but stay the week; I want your support and input. I'll get you a refundable ticket; much cheaper than paying change fees if you need to go back sooner. And pack your running clothes. You'll need the escape as much as I do."

The conversation continued, covering the details needed to leave work and have the neighbor's daughter bring in the mail and feed the cats before drifting into more intimate talk.

When we finally hung up I switched off the small table lamp and lay back on the pillow. I was exhausted, but sleep wouldn't come. My mind played and re-played various scenarios. I tried to picture my own brain shrinking, taking away my essence, my sense of self. I couldn't imagine losing myself that way; who would I be without my memories? I'd once heard someone describe retiring from a lifelong career, one she had deeply identified with, as a form of dying. Was this similar? Was part of Helen's identity dying? I worried about how we were going to get her someplace safe, and what we were going to do with all her possessions, including the house. The responsibility felt overwhelming. It was one thing to be a parent, caring for my own children when they were young. It was quite another to be stepping into someone else's life, an adult's life, especially when that life was slowly disappearing. I hoped I was doing the right thing.

Chapter 19

The to-do list was getting longer: meet with the attorney to have Helen sign paperwork, go to the banks to get added to her accounts, contact Kim for names of places to visit, find a realtor to see what should be done with the house, update my mother on Helen's status, and figure out when I could get back to the Northwest to see clients. If I waited too much longer I'd need to refer them to other therapists. So far they'd all been willing to wait, but I knew their patience, and their need to continue their sessions, would soon become an issue.

I opted to start with the most onerous task first. "Hi, Mom, it's your daughter." I'd learned to identify myself because of her deteriorating hearing; she could no longer recognize me simply by voice. "Wanted to let you know what's going on with Helen."

"Hi, honey, thanks for calling. How is she?" The concern sounded real, but then again, she had once enjoyed acting in amateur theatre. *Would I be this eager to jump in and help her as I have been for Helen?* The thought popped into my head unbidden. The pause that followed was telling. *Wow, what kind of daughter does that make me?*

Her voice snapped me out of my reflection. "Are you still there with her? What's happening?"

I was relieved to focus on something concrete, filling her in on the events of the past week. We talked about the recommendation for moving Helen to a facility, and agreed that was preferable to having anyone in the house.

"So how long do they think she has? Is this something that will go quickly or what? I don't want her to suffer, you know."

I realized I'd been bracing for the inevitable and wasn't disappointed. No matter the subject, whenever we discussed Helen, my mother's jealousy crept in. It was typically hidden in the guise of how close in age they were and how likely it was Helen would outlive her, meaning if she made it to a ripe old age then Mom wouldn't see much of their money. But it was as pointless to get into an argument with her as it was with Helen. The main difference was my mother's mind was still functioning, and, in my opinion, still scheming. I tried to stifle my cynicism and stuck to answering her questions as if they were genuine.

"Mom, Alzheimer's is more of a slow decline than a sudden illness, so we could be talking five to ten years. No one knows. I'm going to do my best to take care of her the way she and Papa Paul had planned. Thankfully, they saved and there are resources. This would be a nightmare otherwise."

Checking the call off my list, I moved to the next item. We were already scheduled to see the attorney on Wednesday, and after he made his assessment we'd go to the bank and brokerage houses. I didn't want to meet with any realtors until we'd found a place for Helen, so assuming things went well with James and the paperwork, the next priority would be visiting facilities.

Finding parking near the law offices was easier than it had been the visit before and we made it without complications. I had coached the receptionist to act as if we were meeting for the first time, not wanting Helen to know I'd already been there. It was important for her to make the decision to work with James, to feel as if it were her choice, which in actuality it was. If she didn't agree, she wouldn't sign anything and I'd have to start over somewhere else.

James came out a few minutes later and introduced himself to Helen, then me. He had dressed in a suit and tie today, perhaps to add an air of formality he thought she might respect. He escorted us back to the same conference room I'd been in the week before. We settled into our seats and spent the next several minutes discussing life in San Toro. Helen was always curious about how long people had lived or worked there, having seen the changes during her forty-six years in the area. She was pleased to discover James had grown up nearby, and that he was familiar with both the Masons and the Roosters, two organizations Papa Paul had been actively involved in. His knowledge gained him credibility with Helen, and I could see that she felt comfortable with him.

"So, Mrs. Allaway, how can I help you today?" James inquired, gently easing her into the purpose of their visit.

Helen and I had already discussed the idea of amending the paperwork for the Trust to add my name and I waited to see if she remembered the reason for the appointment. It was important that Helen understood what was happening. If she didn't, I'd have to go to court to make the changes because it would mean she really wasn't competent. I sat quietly, waiting for her to speak.

"I have a Trust that my granddaughter, or should I say step-granddaughter, is to be in charge of when I die. I want to talk to you about what, if anything, we need to do to add her now. I'm getting older and I think it's a good idea since I'm alone." She paused, and I watched to see if she would tear up at that thought. For the first time since I'd arrived she didn't. "I don't want to have her take over anything; I still want to be in charge. This is a formality you know, just to be smart."

"That's a good idea to plan ahead. We'll make her a Co-Trustee; that keeps you in charge but allows Shelly to help. It makes it easier down the road if it's ever necessary." James's explanation was simple and clear. "We'll just need you to sign a document, get it notarized, which we can do here, and we're good. Would you like me to have my assistant draw up the papers?" I was relieved to see he apparently agreed with the doctor's assessment that Helen knew what she was doing.

Before we left James suggested we stop at the bank and brokerage firm to add my name to those accounts. He told Helen it would give her peace of mind should anything happen, and she readily agreed. I'd already looked up the addresses of the institutions, knowing Helen wouldn't question how I had obtained them. It was another area where my growing knowledge of how Helen's mind functioned was working to my advantage. It helped balance the times when that same mind threatened to drive me crazy.

We finished our remaining errands without any issues. Helen was cooperative and eager to take care of business at both the bank and the brokerage firm. She chatted with the managers about me, how responsible I was, and how it made sense to add me. Despite the awkwardness of being described while I was standing there, I appreciated the kind words and was grateful things had gone so smoothly. Not all days were that easy.

Kim had emailed links to several facility websites, and after perusing them I'd made a list of my top choices. Since meeting with Dr. Scott, Helen was still resisting the idea of having to move, but she was willing to see them, probably in her mind to appease me and prove she didn't belong in one. I didn't really care what her motives were, I was merely glad I didn't have to fight her to get her in the front doors of these places. Maybe she'd actually like one and go voluntarily. *Yeah, and Alan's going to be made the CEO of the company. What's that saying… When pigs fly? About the same chance.* I knew it would never happen, but *hey, a girl can dream, can't she?*

I'd set up appointments at three of the most promising places, and as we climbed into the car Helen offered her opinions about them. "The one at the top of the hill is very luxurious. I think mostly rich people go there. It's got a view of the city and I believe it's very pricey." I'd noticed Helen making similar comments about others, bordering on derogatory in tone, another new behavior. She'd always been very accepting and kind, at least in my presence, and it was shocking to hear the tone in some of her observations. "I doubt I'll like it, but we should look, if only to make you happy. Well, and maybe so I can see what it's like inside. I've only seen it from a distance and I'm curious."

Winding up the steep driveway, Helen filled me in on the history of the growth in this part of town. It had once been the outskirts of San Toro, home to a shopping mall that had brought development with it as the needs of the city grew. The adult living community had been one of several built in the last fifteen or twenty years to address the county's aging population. We both doubted it could be built there today; the views were worth far too much money. I was hopeful the ambience would attract Helen, that our search would be easy if she fell in love with the place.

But as we walked up the bricked path to the entrance I could already sense it wasn't going to be a good fit for Helen, and the tour did nothing to dissuade me. Helen was gracious and complimentary with the marketing agent showing us around, but I couldn't picture her mingling comfortably with the wealth that permeated the facility. High ceilinged formal dining halls, an on-site spa, and an espresso bar weren't necessities she desired. As we moved from the main area housing the common spaces into the apartment wings, I could almost see dollar signs floating out the windows. This place was beyond Helen's budget, but more importantly, it was beyond her style. I could see my mother wanting to come to a place like this, and going to great lengths to convince someone why they should pay for her to do so, but never my grandmother. Going over the admission requirements with the social worker confirmed my decision. The facility required a buy-in, and it was higher than either of us had expected. I wanted a month-to-month deal, not a long-term purchase and re-sale agreement. I'd missed that information on their website. No matter; the two of us had seen, as Helen put it, the highbrow place, and could now cross it off our list. She wouldn't be living here.

Next we visited a lovely church-run place that offered care up to and including a locked dementia unit. We followed our guide through the buildings and were impressed with the antiques decorating the common areas, the completeness of their care, and its proximity to the shopping mall across the street. But as we sat in the office discussing details it was clear they expected Helen to have a full-time caregiver despite living in their facility. That was no better than her having one at home, and a lot more expensive. As the administrator walked us to the front door I promised we would think things over and get back to her. It was always easier to say no in a voice mail.

We stopped for coffee at a strip mall near the last facility on the list. Helen needed a rest, and it gave us a chance to talk about what we'd seen. We'd both deleted the one on the hill immediately, but I was curious to hear Helen's reaction to the Lutheran home. While I didn't relish the added expense of a caregiver, they did have the locked dementia unit, meaning Helen wouldn't have to move if it ever became necessary for that level of care. I avoided pointing that out to her, however. It was something for me to appreciate and Helen to forget.

"That place was beautiful; I loved all the furniture and the paintings. It was elegant, but not like the one on the hill. It felt more welcoming in some ways, but it also felt rather cold. Did you notice the residents all wore nametags, as if the people there didn't know who they were?" she shuddered. "That was creepy. And the locked unit! Did you see the people in there? They were all sitting around, heads drooping, not saying anything, like zombies! I don't belong there!" She was adamant, and I had no reason to disagree. I'd felt the same way myself.

"No, you don't belong there for sure. That's for folks who really can't take care of themselves, ones who need to be in a nursing home. You aren't in need of that, and I doubt you ever will be." I wanted to reassure her, to keep her from refusing to look anyplace else. "Let's finish up your hot chocolate and go see the next one. Fingers crossed we both like it."

When we were ready to go, I took her hand as we crossed the parking lot, noticing once more how soft her delicate skin felt against mine.

The car had warmed up in the sunshine, and I rolled the driver's side window down to help it cool off. It was only a short drive to our destination, not enough for the air conditioner to do its magic. I helped Helen buckle her seatbelt, something else I noticed she had begun to struggle with, another small detail that could only been picked up on in person, not over the phone.

Unlike the two previous places we'd visited, Duncan House was modest and unassuming from the front. The neighborhood boulevard that led to the facility was lined by a row of shade trees, providing a screen from the traffic and softening the otherwise plain stucco wall of the older building. There was no fancy front lobby or ornate driveway, just a parking lot along the side with neatly marked stalls, the ones in the front for staff. Closer to what I assumed were the resident apartments, the spaces were wider and filled with well-maintained cars, the type most grandparents used: a bit larger, a bit more staid, and a lot safer for older drivers. One exception popped into my mind: Papa Paul and his sporty T-birds.

He'd always loved the iconic car.

I found a spot and parked. Like Alan, I'd gotten into the habit of opening the door for Helen, making it easier for her to get in and out. "First impressions?" I asked as we stood next to the car, taking in the surroundings. It already felt better, less pretentious and more approachable. I hoped it was as inviting on the inside.

"Comfortable," she replied. "A lot less snooty than the one on the hill, and I don't see anyone drooling yet." I appreciated that she hadn't lost her sense of humor.

The lobby was friendly and inviting, with a number of small seating groups spread across a well-lit room. Several of the couches were occupied by comfortably dressed women chatting and sipping coffee. A few metal walkers stood nearby, and voices raised and lowered most likely depending upon the quality of the listener's hearing aids. No one wore nametags except the staff, a few of whom we witnessed stopping and having animated conversations with the residents. The place felt lived in, homey, somewhere I could imagine Helen staying. I only hoped she felt the same.

"Hi, I'm Shelly Johnson, and this is my grandmother, Helen Allaway. We're here to take a tour," I introduced myself to the woman behind the front desk. "I think Natalie is going to meet with us?"

"Yes, she's expecting you. I'll let her know you're here; she'll only be a minute. Would you like a coffee while you're waiting?" The receptionist reinforced my first impressions of approachability.

"Thanks, we're good. We'll wait for her over here," I replied, gently guiding Helen to one of the seating groupings. We were soon joined by Natalie, a petite sandy-haired woman who appeared to be in her late forties, tastefully dressed in street clothes, not a uniform like the previous facility. Introducing herself as the resident manager, she took a seat across from us. She engaged Helen in small talk before asking her to describe herself and why she was considering Duncan House.

"I'm being forced to give up my home. I don't really want to move, but I am lonely so far out. Maybe I would like it better being around people. I really am a people person. My partner was taken away; they said I couldn't take care of him." She paused, her eyes moistening. "I took good care of him; I didn't do anything wrong." Her voice trailed off. She was all over the place with her answers, defensive one second, reflective the next. She went on for several minutes, pausing when her emotions threatened to overwhelm her. I was grateful she didn't burst into uncontrollable rages or torrents of tears. Perhaps the frequent repetition of her story was helping her make sense of it, or maybe she was just growing tired of hearing it herself.

I listened quietly as Natalie queried Helen about various aspects of her life, particularly her years as a nurse. *She's good. She knows how to get Helen to like her, and if Helen likes Natalie, she may like Duncan House.* Natalie gently steered the conversation to Helen's loneliness, zeroing in on her lack of transportation and the isolation from others her age. Helen nodded in agreement, sharing how much she missed being able to drive into town and how trapped she felt. She asked if Bruce could come live with her, if Myron would let him. She was about to go off on one of her typical tangents, complaining about Myron's treatment of her when Natalie deftly changed the subject, asking if we'd like to take a tour.

"Let's start here in the main building." As we walked she directed her descriptions of the various amenities to Helen, which I appreciated. "Here's the library. A lot of our residents come here in the evenings to socialize and watch TV. We show movies on the weekends, and over here are the mailboxes." She pointed out an alcove filled with locked, numbered boxes. "You get your own mail, and we put any notices in the slot for your newspaper if you get one delivered. We also have a machine here for coffee, tea, and hot chocolate that you can use anytime."

We moved into the dining room, which was being set for dinner. "We serve a simple menu at lunch where you can pick what you'd like from a small sampling of offerings, perhaps a hot dish, a sandwich choice, or some type of salad. For dinner, as you can see, we put out tablecloths, linen napkins, and candles. You choose your meal from a menu, with three options each evening such as steak, fish, or a chicken dish. The servers bring it to your table, along with a glass of white or red wine if you care to have one."

Helen had wandered over to the wall of full-length windows. "What a lovely garden! I love my yard. I've always enjoyed working outside."

Natalie joined her. "Then let's go see it." She led the way out of the dining hall to a side door. Holding it open for us, she gave us time to step out and explore the space. Surrounded on three sides by buildings, the landscapers had created a tiny sanctuary for residents to spend time outdoors. A few rooms had private patios, separated by wrought iron fences and plantings. The covered deck backed up to the dining room, and the far wall was covered in vines. I'm sure it is stunning in the spring and summer when everything is in full bloom. I could definitely see Helen spending time out here.

"Let's move on to the apartments," Natalie said, taking us back inside. "We have two buildings, this one and one in back, with private residences, one and two bedroom units. They all have kitchenettes, but most residents eat in the dining room. We provide housecleaning and laundry weekly, but we also have laundry rooms on each floor if you want to do your own."

After climbing the stairs to the second floor, she led us to a door halfway down the hall. "This is our one-bedroom," she said as she unlocked the door and walked in. "The kitchenette has a two-burner stove and a refrigerator. As you can see, it has an open counter to connect to the living room. Over here is the bedroom and bath. Each room has a call button in case of emergency, and you can decorate however you like." She stepped into the kitchen to give us a chance to walk around by ourselves.

"What do you think?" I asked Helen as we stood in the small but well-lit bedroom. "Can you imagine living here? The people sure are nice compared to the other two places!" Natalie had introduced us to various staff members as we met them on the tour. She made a point of mentioning the low turnover rate, commenting that most staff had been there upwards of five years. That, I knew, spoke well of the working conditions. It was also reassuring that Helen would have consistency as her memory declined.

"This apartment is far too small. How in the world would I fit my things in here? Where would I put my sewing machine? Where would I have room for a guest? Where will you sleep when you visit?" She was full of questions. I doubted she had used her sewing machine in ten or more years, but it was suddenly a concern.

"Why don't we look at the two-bedroom unit?" I wanted to move on before she made an irreversible decision. "Natalie said there was one in the other building. Maybe that will be large enough."

The back building housed a small computer room on the main floor. Natalie extolled the convenience of having a workstation available for the residents, but that feature was lost on Helen. Even when her memory was perfect she had never understood modern technology. All her letters were written by hand, and the travel journals she treasured had been typed on Papa Paul's electric typewriter, using carbon paper to create duplicates.

We rode the elevator to the second floor and followed Natalie down the long hall to the far end. She unlocked the door and waited while we stepped inside. The floor plan was similar to the one we'd just seen, but instead of an alcove leading to the bath and bedroom there was a hallway. We passed the bathroom before arriving at what I assumed was the second bedroom. It was about the size of the guest room at Helen's house, with a small window opened to a row of trees blocking the view of the condo development just beyond. Helen glanced around and then led the way to the other room. It was hard to categorize as the master since it was only slightly larger and had no private bath, but it did have larger windows that faced a vast undeveloped expanse. The view swept up the hillside, currently displaying the browned grasses so common this time of year. The feeling was of serenity; the space was peaceful and quiet. We stood looking out for several minutes.

"Can you see yourself here?" I finally broke the silence. "I love this view. Not as many plants as your place, but it's almost as private. And the spare room would give you the space you want. I think it's a pretty good set-up."

"It is nice," Helen admitted. "But I don't know how I'll fit everything in here. I want my sewing machine and the trundle bed you're using." She turned and walked back into the living room where Natalie waited.

"I don't want to come here, but if they insist, then I want this apartment." I heard a tinge of resignation in her voice. I was ecstatic that Helen had found a place.

Natalie led us back to the lobby where we returned to the couches in the corner. She left momentarily to get the paperwork Helen needed to sign to hold the space and forms for her doctors to fill out. I had suggested Helen bring her checkbook for just this reason, and as she filled out the deposit she seemed more excited than I'd seen her in days. She actually looked pleased to be moving, commenting repeatedly about how lonely she would be in the house alone.

Chapter 20

"Shelly, this is Natalie from Duncan House. I was wondering why Helen cancelled the check she wrote yesterday. We went to deposit it and were told it had been stopped. Can you fill me in?"

I had gotten in the habit of taking my cell phone with me on my runs, stuffing it into the small pouch on the back of my tights in case Helen needed something while I was out. I was glad I'd thought to give this number to Natalie.

"Actually, no, I have no idea what's going on. I'm not at the house right now, but I can find out when I get back and give you a call. She's still coming, so please don't do anything with the apartment." I was concerned it might get rented out from under us; there was only one two-bedroom available, and I knew there was no way I'd get Helen into anything smaller. She didn't actually need the space, but psychologically she thought she did, and if that's what it took to get her to move then that's what we'd rent. Better to get her there and deal with moving her into the right space later. Getting her out of the house was the first goal.

"Helen, did you do something with the check to Duncan House?" I came in and sat down in the living room where Helen was reading the paper. "There seems to be some confusion about being able to cash it." Remembering some of our earlier interactions, I kept my voice calm, curious rather than accusatory.

"Yes, I know exactly what happened. I called the bank last night and told them I didn't want that check to go through. I don't want to move. The place is fine, but I'm not going." She turned back to her paper, the conversation over.

"But you can't just decide to stay here. Remember what Dr. Scott said? Neither of us wants the state to put you somewhere, and we both liked Duncan House. You even said it was nice to be around people, that you're lonely here. You'll have your own furniture there, so it will be familiar. I promise it'll be okay."

"Why do I have to go?"

And so we went round and round again before she finally gave in. I had the feeling we'd re-visit this more than once before we got her moved. Like Alan, I sometimes wanted to take notes and pictures of everything to prove I wasn't going crazy. I was living in Wonderland with a constantly shifting reality, one I couldn't control. My only choice was to accept it.

"After I shower, we need to go into town to drop off another check at Duncan House." I headed down the hall before Helen could protest.

When I emerged from the bathroom half an hour later I was pleased to find Helen dressed and ready to go. I was becoming accustomed to these swings in functioning, but it was always a relief when she appeared focused and normal. At the same time it caused me to question the diagnosis; maybe it was just exhaustion. But then I'd remember the conversation with Dr. Scott and the images of Helen's brain; he'd described the experience of Alzheimer's patients' minds as being like Swiss cheese.

"Imagine it having gaps throughout, some small, some quite large. But there are also a lot of areas without any holes. Sometimes they're able to navigate without falling into any of them, and they seem fine. But then they trip and fall, and aren't able to find a way out of the hole. They loop and spin, trying to escape, but they can't. It's our job to throw them a lifeline, a way out of the spiral. Deflection, changing the subject, almost anything but direct confrontation helps." It was a good mental image; sometimes Helen walked between the spaces and appeared her old self, but then she'd fall into one of the growing gaps and be lost. I had become her lifeline.

We had one stop to make before grabbing lunch, and that was back at Duncan House. I'd asked Helen to write out a second check and hand it to me for safekeeping. We met briefly with Natalie, who wanted confirmation from Helen that she did intend to come before accepting the deposit. We scheduled the move-in date for a couple of weeks later, as soon as the apartment was ready for a new tenant.

Chapter 21

Alan's arrival late Friday evening shifted us into the next phase of the transition. Helen had a place to live, and we'd taken care of the business dealings with banks and the Trust. We now had to decide what to do with the house. I knew Helen wasn't ready to sell it; she believed she might return to it someday and there was no reason to dispel that notion, at least not yet.

Neither Alan nor I relished the idea of becoming landlords, let alone long-distance ones, and we didn't have any such experience. Seeking advice on an agent we could trust, I called Molly for a recommendation. I'd kept her apprised of our plans as they'd unfolded so she wasn't surprised by the request.

"The guy we used, Dennis, was actually good. He helped us sort out some of the problems we ran into and was quick to answer our calls. I think he handles leasing as well as selling, so he might be a good place to start," Molly offered. "I hate to see Helen leave, but I agree with you that she clearly needs help."

"If nothing else, it will buy us time to see how it goes," I said. I could hear rustling in the background.

"Okay, found his number. Ready?" Molly inquired.

"Fire away," I replied, jotting his name and the office number down on a small slip of paper. "I'll keep you posted. Thanks for the info." We chatted a few more minutes before hanging up.

Dennis answered on the second ring, and I briefly filled him in on our needs. I was thrilled to find out he not only lived in the same neighborhood, but his parents had been friends with my grandparents. After going over the details he offered to handle the leasing of the house in exchange for a flat fee, a percentage of a month's rent, and he'd keep an eye on the house for no charge, calling if there was a problem. I knew it was probably because he hoped we'd use him if we chose to sell in the future, but I couldn't believe my good fortune, and only hoped he turned out to be as honest as he came across over the phone. I arranged to have him come by once Helen had moved; I didn't want her there while we discussed what needed to be done to make it attractive to tenants.

"How do you dismantle a house that someone has lived in for over forty years?" Alan whispered. We were still in bed, having one of the few private conversations we could sneak in with Helen around. "They have so much crap!"

I wasn't sure I'd describe years of travel memories as crap, but the amount of stuff was overwhelming. Adding to it was the evidence of Helen's dementia: not only had she accumulated frozen vegetables and newspapers, I'd found stacks of toilet paper, cleaning supplies, and canned goods in the basement. She also had a closet full of items from years of entertaining: plastic plates, table linens, paper streamers in various colors, candles; and an endless scattering throughout the house of scraps of paper, all with notes scribbled in tiny, almost unreadable handwriting, with numerous erasures and crossed out words. The list was endless.

"One box at a time?" I smiled. "And hopefully she won't unpack them all during the night."

"That's not funny." Alan shuddered.

"It may not be funny, but we have to laugh or we'll go nuts. Trust me on that; you haven't been here for two weeks straight like I have. She's wonderful in many ways, but she wears me out. I feel so bad for her, but it's still hard to be with her twenty-four seven. The advantage of her being in a facility is that lots of people are there to interact with her. Here it's just been me." We talked quietly for the next few minutes before it was finally time to get up. We got dressed and headed into the kitchen to face another day.

"Why don't we begin to sort through some of your clothes, separating what you think you might need from items you don't wear anymore." It seemed like a reasonable place to start, less threatening than dismantling pieces of Helen's house. Each knick-knack represented a memory, and keeping those in place as long as possible felt important. I didn't think clothes would carry the same meaning as the souvenirs. Once again, I was proven wrong.

"I remember sewing this jacket for a trip we took to Poland after your grandfather retired. I made all my own clothes then so we could save money for our trips. I took that Stretch and Sew class because the knits travelled much better than other materials." Helen was having no problems recalling the minutest details of each outfit I pulled from the closet. I doubted she'd ever disposed of a single blouse, skirt, or pair of pants. She had been so proud not only of her sewing talents, but her ability to make clothes to fit her tiny frame. She frequently commented on her flat chest, big hips and bowed legs, and finding things tailored to her unique figure had been a struggle until that Stretch and Sew class. Now I was asking her to sort through her treasures and get rid of many of them.

"What if we put some things in storage, and you get them out whenever you need them? We'll be getting a unit anyway to keep some of the furniture in case you decide you might want it." Alan and I had already come up with that strategy to help with the transition. "We can buy those wardrobe boxes that'll keep everything in good shape."

"Well, I do switch out clothes for summer and winter, so that might work. There are probably some things I can toss or donate, things I don't really wear anymore." Helen's response was more accommodating than I had hoped.

I sent Alan out to purchase boxes while Helen and I began the sorting process. Most of the clothes in the closet were for summer; the winter wardrobe was in the guest room Alan and I shared. We started in Helen's room, making several piles that we packed into boxes when Alan returned. The process went well for the first hour, but then Helen's attention waned and she soon found excuses to keep me from the task. It reminded me of when the kids were little and I tried to get them to clean their rooms. Suddenly David wanted to show his latest LEGO structure or Janie begged me to look at the library book with the pictures of ponies. Helen went into the office and took out travel books, wanting to show me photos of a trip to Antarctica, or headed into the kitchen 'for a quick snack' despite having eaten only a short while before. I'd seen a picture showing the arc of a lifespan: from toddler to teen to adult to old age. The toddler and elderly images were remarkably alike, implying the return to dependence in the final years. I'd always viewed it as comical, but now it wasn't quite as amusing.

While I attempted to corral Helen, repeatedly bringing her back into the bedroom and her clothes, Alan waded through the items in the office. The desk had been cleared of Bruce's papers, files and folders, but the cabinets contained a variety of books and knickknacks that belonged to Papa Paul and had never been sorted after his passing. Occasionally Alan came into the bedroom where Helen and I were debating the merits of one pair of pants versus another. His interruptions often triggered an emotional response in

Helen, but we both felt it was important for her to be included in most of the decisions we were making.

"Helen, I found this behind the safe. I started to read it and realized it's too personal. It looks like a collection of poems or letters Papa Paul wrote to you." He handed the small blue binder to her. "I think this is something you'll want to keep."

Helen reached out and took it. She opened it to the first page, revealing my grandfather's familiar neat handwriting. I watched as she read, tears running silently down her cheeks.

"He always wrote me love letters and poems," she said softly. "He was constantly telling me how much I meant to him, and how happy he was that we met. I never had his gift for words." She went to the nightstand and pulled out a Kleenex, wiping her eyes before sitting down on the bed. We watched for a moment as she slowly turned the pages and then Alan tapped me gently on the sleeve, nodding his head toward the door. We left Helen alone to her memories.

"Oh my God," Alan said as we sat down at the kitchen table. "What he wrote was incredible. It took me a few pages to understand what I was looking at, and the love just poured out."

'I know all you've lived through, the secrets you've kept hidden from others, afraid of and condemnations'... 'I love every part of your being'... 'You are the best thing that ever happened in my life' ... 'you make me feel so safe and secure.'

"You get the idea. No wonder she was so protective of him, of their relationship. What an amazing love they must have had. I only wish I'd met him; I think I would have really like him."

"Yeah, you definitely would have liked each other. It's too bad I married the wrong husband first," I teased. "But I'm glad you found that book. I think it'll bring back a lot of happy memories for Helen, especially now that she's still so distraught over Bruce's leaving. I hope he can come back when she gets to Duncan House, though. Being alone isn't good for her."

We sat in silence, each lost in our own thoughts, giving Helen privacy for a few more minutes. Finally Alan pushed back his chair, signaling the break was over.

"Okay, that's probably long enough. Let's see if we can get her to pack a few more things before we give up for the day." He slid the chair back into place and headed down the hall, me following closely behind.

Chapter 22

I couldn't imagine spending the next few weeks in San Toro waiting for the new apartment to be ready. I was feeling a lot of pressure to return to the office and clients, and there wasn't much we could do in the house until Helen was out. Every time we started to pack she found a way to avoid the task, although thankfully, she didn't remove items from boxes. However, she did become stubborn and obstinate whenever either of us tried to help her focus on sorting clothes or deciding which items she wanted to put into storage.

"I imagine it's like watching someone dismantle your life in front of your eyes," I said to Alan. We were out for a run together, a rare opportunity to be alone. Helen had encouraged us to go after breakfast and we quickly took her up on the offer. We ran through the quiet streets out to the main boulevard that curved along the bay, finding the path that hugged the lapping water. The tide was in, nearly touching the short seawall, as we kept up a comfortable, conversational pace.

"How can you be okay seeing everything you've ever done, everything you've worked for, reduced to what will fit in a few boxes," I continued. "I know it's just stuff, but it's stuff that represents her entire life. It's bad enough her brain is shrinking;

now her world is as well. I wish I could be absolutely certain we're doing the right thing. Intellectually I know we are, but I feel so damn guilty."

We reached the old rock quarry, the turnaround point on my solo runs, but I wasn't ready to quit. "Let's keep going. It feels good to be out here, away from everything for even a few minutes. We can always walk to cool off if we get tired."

"Works for me," Alan agreed. We ran in silence for a while, enjoying the quiet and the scenery.

"I've been thinking about the next few weeks," Alan began, as we walked the final few blocks home. "You need to get back to your clients, I need to show my face at work, and we're going to have to come back here again when it's time to move Helen and take care of the house. Any ideas how we can pull that off?"

"I've been wondering the same thing. What do you think about using a service to bring someone into the house? Kim mentioned them in case we decided to go that route. How about I call her and get some names? Helen will hate it, but then again, she may welcome the companionship if we leave. She's getting used to me being here even though she's constantly reminding me she'd be fine alone."

"Okay, call Kim on Monday. We'll keep packing, or at least making vain attempts at packing, until then. Maybe that's something we can have the caregiver help with, someone more detached than we are. Give them something to do, to stay busy. We can come back on the weekends to show Helen we haven't abandoned her." Alan was always optimistic. I had my doubts, but I really wanted to get home, and this was the best shot I had.

Kim suggested getting together in person at the same Starbucks. With Alan around it was easier to get out of the house, and I welcomed the chance to talk freely. Once again Kim brought a stack of papers, this time with names and profiles of several agencies in the area that provided home care services. After exchanging pleasantries and ordering drinks, she inquired about Helen.

"From your call it sounds like a lot's been happening. I'm impressed with what you've been able to accomplish in such a short time. How is she handling all of this, and more importantly, how're you doing?" She sat back and took a sip of her tea. "This has to be really hard on you."

"I'm on auto-pilot. I keep making lists and focusing on the immediate task, which helps. Sometimes I get overwhelmed, especially when I look at all of this through Helen's eyes, although I'm not sure what she's experiencing is what I think she's experiencing. Hard not to project how I'd be doing if it were my brain. I can't fathom having my memory disappearing, losing myself piece by piece. Who will she become?" I felt a welling of emotion as I pictured some of Helen's confusion over what seemed such simple things.

"I've worked for a long time with families dealing with this, and I don't think it ever gets easy. What I can share is that there are stages she'll most likely go through. Some people deny it, some get angry, while others seem more accepting. For many, the personality before the diagnosis becomes more exaggerated: if Helen tended to have bursts of anger when frustrated, then it's not surprising she's reacting with anger now. While it may become more challenging for you, it may become easier for her as she loses more of her memory. She'll stop fighting the loss of control and her new world will become her new reality. Most clients I've seen who initially struggle do find peace over time. It doesn't mean there won't be other challenges, and there are many, but her anger should dissipate. It can be somewhat hellish until then; wish I could say different. But you also describe her as loving and kind, and you'll probably see that as well. In some ways it's harder on the family, because the person you knew is disappearing. If you're able to accept the new person she becomes, then it's easier for you."

I appreciated Kim's candor and insight. It supported what I'd been learning in the book Dr. Campbell had recommended. The book offered a compassionate look at what was going on inside the world of Alzheimer's patients and gave concrete suggestions as to how to meet them where they were instead of trying to make them confront a reality they no longer experienced. It didn't always make it any easier to be with Helen, but it did make it more understandable. The challenge was learning to let go of explanations as a way of getting cooperation and instead being comfortable with compliance without understanding.

"So let's talk about temporary solutions for you to get home." Kim leafed through the papers on the table. "There are a few different options; agencies and private nurses are the ones used most frequently. The advantage of an agency is there are multiple people on staff so if one doesn't work out the agency can send someone else. That may be a good choice for Helen, given her difficulty with having anyone in the house. However, a private nurse may be more skilled and able to deal with her moods. But it takes time to interview and find a good fit, which sounds like a problem with you wanting to leave."

"Tell me about the agencies. Which ones do you like, what are the pros and cons of each? I think given the short timeline to get someone onboard, and the brief duration we're going to need someone, that's the better choice."

We spent the next half hour discussing the strengths of each company, and which might be the best resource both for Helen and for me. I settled on Happy Helpers, an agency that checked off several of the boxes I determined would be important: a larger staff, a long time presence in the area, a solid reputation, and the ability to send caregivers to Duncan House should the need arise once Helen moved. Continuity mattered; anything to reduce her confusion.

"There's something else you may want to consider going forward, and that is hiring a care manager since you won't be here all the time." Kim pulled out another sheet from her pile. "I brought these names in case you want to think about it." She handed it across the table.

"What's a care manager?" Another new concept; I was getting quite an education.

"Essentially they function as you when you aren't here, but you can use them however works best. Some do everything, such as handle all the interactions with medical providers, deal with staff, hire and supervise any caregivers she may need; it's up to you. Others primarily oversee things from more of a distance, but are there in emergencies until you can be reached. If nothing else, their presence reminds the facility that Helen hasn't been abandoned, that she has family keeping an eye on her. I hate to say it, but no matter where someone is, no matter how good the place is, if no one ever checks in, it seems to affect how someone is treated. I think it's an unconscious reaction; if nobody else cares, why should I go out of my way?"

"I get that, as much as it sucks. I definitely don't want anyone to infer that I don't care because I live out of state. Helen is just so adamant about not leaving here." After talking further, I left the meeting more overwhelmed than when I had arrived.

Chapter 23

The next few days were a flurry of activity, calling agencies, interviewing potential caregivers, and repeatedly explaining our plans to Helen. She vehemently opposed having anyone in the house, but was forced to relent when given no choice. This became the default position: Helen argued, Alan or I repeatedly explained, and Helen ultimately acquiesced. Alan was quite persuasive dealing with her anger, staying calm and focused, answering her questions over, and over, and over, again. It was painful for all of us and I kept wishing it would somehow get better.

We all finally agreed on Marie, a student in her early thirties who worked part time to support herself in graduate school, and Laney, an older woman who had been providing care for several years and understood the demands of clients with Alzheimer's. The two women would alternate twenty-four hour shifts, sleeping in the guest room and helping Helen pack during the day.

Plans in place, we booked our flight back to Seattle for Sunday afternoon. I called Molly to fill her in and ask if she could be available in an emergency, to which she readily agreed. I then emailed clients and began scheduling appointments beginning Monday morning. After living with Helen, the idea of a regular workweek was appealing. I relished the idea of neat hour-long sessions, dinner at home, and sleeping in my own bed. Knowing I was leaving Helen in good hands made the thought of going home even sweeter.

Once the details for the next weeks were set, I tried to get back to packing. It continued in fits and starts, mostly with Helen finding excuses to avoid it. The lone exception to her resistance came when we spent an afternoon sorting through boxes of personal papers we'd stumbled upon in the back of Papa Paul's office closet. It was filled with correspondence he'd saved over the years.

"I had no idea he made copies of the letters he wrote," I muttered as I examined each sheet of thin typing paper with the telltale blue ink indicating he'd used carbon paper. "And I had no idea he kept every letter I ever wrote him, not to mention those from Mom and Gary. There's quite a history here!"

"He had me type a lot of his letters, and as you know he was a collector, so these were just part of what he collected," Helen explained. "I think he also wanted to document his life story. Maybe he thought he'd be famous within the family," she chuckled. "Or maybe it was just his business training to save it all; in any case, there's a lot here."

I dug through the box, finding piles of letters as far back as the late fifties. One particular missive caught my eye. I pulled it out and began reading:

Dear Ann,

I was surprised by your latest letter, and especially by the vehemence in which you attacked me. I have always endeavored to take care of you well beyond the time you should have been able to care for yourself.

You complain I have never helped you out financially and haven't supported you in your desires. I do not believe I have shorted you in any way, and have sent you generous amounts of money numerous times when you cried out for help. But I also believe you will always find yourself in another crisis and want more, promising always to change but never following through. I have lived my life in a prudent manner, never buying things I cannot afford, while I see you 'needing' things that are far outside your budget.

I am no longer willing to indulge your irresponsibility. I will no longer be a bank you can draw upon in your manufactured emergencies. I fervently hope you will learn to manage a dollar and take care of yourself and your children in a responsible manner.

You are and will always be my beloved daughter. I wring my hands at times wondering what else I could have done to teach you the value of a dollar. Perhaps I have failed in my obligations, but I must now put a halt to this.

Love,

Papa

I was stunned. I'd had conversations with Papa Paul and Helen regarding my mom's constant seeking of money, but this was a more direct rebuttal than anything I'd expected. I noticed the date on the letter: September 23, 1958. It had been going on far longer than I'd thought. Shuffling through the box, I found at least a dozen more letters of a similar vein, dated randomly across several decades. Papa Paul had held the line he'd established, but her pleas hadn't ceased, nor had their tone: using guilt by blaming him for her parents' divorce despite it being her mother who had initiated it, for criticizing her career choices, or basically for any reason she could find. When he did send financial gifts for birthdays or Christmas, her responses were filled with gratitude that she could finally pay off whatever her current disaster was. It was clear it wasn't just me she'd been constantly pestering; I began to suspect it was anyone who might cough up something with the right story.

"Helen, I had no idea Mom harassed you this often for money. I didn't realize it was so relentless and for such large sums. I remember her saying you had forbidden Papa Paul from helping her out, refusing to 'buy her children jackets when they were on the verge of freezing one winter.' She kept repeating that story to anyone who would listen. But she always made you out as the bad guy, not Papa Paul."

"She never approved of me," Helen stated. "I understand how hard it must have been for her when we first got together. After all, I was only five years older than her when I came along. She was in her mid-twenties, a newly divorced single parent with two small children. For years I did everything I could to be friends and smooth things over, and on the surface it seemed to work, but underneath she never accepted me. She's always resented me, felt I took her father from her."

Helen picked a booklet out of the box. "This is from a reunion your grandfather and I went to at the Children's Home where I'd lived," she commented. "I saw quite a few of the girls I knew back then. It was a lovely place despite it being essentially an orphanage. The people were very kind, and it was in a good neighborhood with good schools. We all made good lives for ourselves. The home did a remarkable job of raising proper young women." Other than the one night in the hospital, Helen didn't usually open up about those early years. I waited to see if she'd reveal more.

"My mother never came to visit, only my father. He was wonderful." She paged though the book before returning it to the box.

"Are you hungry?" The abrupt subject change startled me despite the weeks of being subjected to Helen's randomness. I'd been enjoying the normalcy of our conversation. It felt like the old Helen for those few moments, but now reality reappeared. I neatened the papers on the floor before adding them to the box and carrying it to my bedroom. This was one I wanted to keep and go through more leisurely later.

Chapter 24

Sunday finally arrived, and Marie was taking her first shift. She knocked on the front door with plenty of time for us to get her settled and still make it to the airport. We'd worried Helen might renege on her willingness to have someone in the home, but she seemed calm and comfortable as we carried our bags down to the car and came up to say our goodbyes.

"We'll be back in a week," I reminded her. "Marie and Laney have my number and you can call anytime." I exchanged a few last minute instructions with Marie, hugged and kissed Helen, and stood back as Alan did the same. Waving as we went down the front steps, we got into the car and pulled away.

"Man, my head is bouncing all over the place," I said as we turned onto the freeway onramp. "I can't believe I'm going home, even if it's for only a week, but I feel horrid leaving Helen. She seemed to like Marie, but it still feels crappy leaving her with someone she doesn't know. I hope we're doing the right thing."

Alan glanced over from the driver's seat. "We'll never really know what the right thing is; we just have to do our best. It's new for all of us. You've been wonderful to Helen, and I think she realizes that even in her current state. She trusts you." His words were reassuring, but doubts still remained.

The first call came early the next morning. "Shelly, I don't like Marie. She has funny eyes and keeps staring at me. I don't want her here. You need to have her leave," Helen whispered into the phone. I pictured her huddled on the bed, door closed and her hand covering the receiver, afraid of being overheard.

"Helen, I don't think she's staring at you. She has no reason to do that. I think she's fine; you liked her a lot when we interviewed her." I tried to reason with her. "In any case, Laney will be coming at noon to stay with you tonight. That'll give you a break. You liked her as well, so maybe you'll feel better."

"No, I don't want Marie here again. She's got weird eyes. I think she's watching every move I make. I don't want her around." I knew it was pointless to argue.

"Well, as I said, Laney will be there soon, and Marie will be going home." I glanced at the clock. "Helen, I have to go see a client right now, but I think you'll enjoy spending time with Laney."

"Well I don't have much choice, do I?" Her voice was tinged with anger. "That damn doctor thinking I need someone here."

"I know, it doesn't make sense to you, but we don't want to get in trouble with the state so we have to do this. It won't be long until you can move into Duncan House and I think you'll like that a lot more. I have to go now, I love you," I said with a finality in my voice.

"Fine. Goodbye." I was growing accustomed to Helen's moodiness, and the fact that it probably would be forgotten the next time we talked. It was one of the few benefits of the disease.

The calls continued, sometimes four and five times a day. Helen had a myriad of complaints about the caregivers, and I patiently listened to each of them, reassuring her that she'd soon be moving and would no longer need them. I reminded her that this was why she had decided to go to Duncan House, so she wouldn't have to have people in her home. She'd calm down, only to become upset later and call again. I doubted she even remembered that we'd spoken sometimes only an hour earlier.

She didn't want anyone there, and I could understand that. I wouldn't want a stranger living with me, either. But I didn't want her left alone, even if she could manage to care for herself, which I doubted. If she got the idea that I trusted her for a few days, then why would she need to move? I certainly didn't want to open that door; the arguments would never cease.

The week passed quickly. Clients were glad to have sessions, and it felt better connecting with them in person to fill them in on what I expected might happen over the next month or so as we moved my grandmother into a care facility and prepared the house for leasing. Alan and I hoped to work weekdays and fly to San Toro on the weekends, getting as much done as possible during the short visits.

After our arrival late Friday afternoon, Helen spent an hour complaining bitterly about both Marie and Laney. Yet when we first showed up, and Marie was still there, the four of us chatted for a few minutes and Helen appeared to have genuinely enjoyed Marie's company. Which version of the story was true?

Rather than attempting to get Helen to pack, a task which had been no more successful with the caregivers than it had been with us the week before, we opted to spend Saturday driving through the wine country north of town. We knew Helen loved car trips and we weren't in the mood for two days of struggle. We'd figure out the packing somehow; it wasn't worth fighting when Helen was already unhappy with Marie and Laney in the house.

We stopped to eat in one of the small towns that dotted the area, choosing a quaint restaurant off the main square. Helen stopped at an artsy storefront to look in the window. I nudged Alan aside, taking the opportunity to whisper to him.

"We need to make sure Helen is seated facing us and not the other diners. Trust me on this."

"Why? He looked at me, puzzled.

"I forgot to tell you. At Starbucks one day, she made a couple of really loud, inappropriate comments about others. Things like 'look at that man's giant nose, you know, the Jewish man there.' She covered her mouth as if she were whispering, but then almost yelled at me. It was mortifying, and so unlike her. I've never heard her say anything remotely like it before."

Alan glanced at Helen, still enthralled by the displays. "Maybe along with her memory all her filters are going, too. Well, good to know." He went up to her, gently putting his arm around her.

"I'm hungry, let's go eat," he said and led her to the restaurant. As the greeter showed us to our table, Alan unobtrusively pulled out a chair for Helen that faced the wall.

Chapter 25

Helen hadn't talked much about Marie or Laney since that first hour after our arrival, which we took as a good sign that the following week would be an improvement. That notion was quickly dispelled when we mentioned needing to remake the bed for Laney's return Sunday afternoon before we headed back to the airport.

"Don't leave me, don't leave me," Helen begged. "Don't go, don't make me stay!" She burst into tears, looking as if she might crumble and fall to the floor. "Don't leave me here!"

I was stunned. I'd never seen this panicky type of behavior in Helen. I moved to her side, wrapping my arms around her as if she were a small child afraid to be left with a babysitter for the first time. Helen clung to me, crying and pleading to go with us. No amount of soothing calmed her. I glanced at Alan. "Can we take her?" I mouthed.

"I don't think we have a choice," he whispered.

"Helen, would you like to come with us to Seattle for a little vacation?" He came over next to her. "We'd love to have you visit with us. The kids would be so happy to see you."

Helen looked up. "Really? Go with you? Not stay here?" She wiped her eyes with her hand. "Really? You mean it? I don't have to stay here with those awful women? Yes, yes, I'll go with you!" Her body relaxed into my arms, and relief spread rapidly across her face. She hugged me tightly before letting go and reaching out to Alan. He held her for several minutes as she kept repeating over and over, "You are such a dear man. Thank you."

I jumped into full organizational mode. "I'll check with the airlines to see if another seat is available or if we have to take a different flight. If we hustle we can still make it. I'll pack Helen's clothes. Alan, can you cancel Happy Helpers?" I took a breath. "Helen, you have a driver's license, right? You'll need it to fly. Let's hope it's still current. If not, we have a problem."

I found Helen's wallet, her license inside, with an expiration date still two years from now. Relieved, I called the airline and spoke to an agent, explaining the situation. She wasn't able to find a seat next to ours, but we were able to get her on the same flight and change the seat assignments so that Helen would sit with me and Alan would sit alone. We sorted through the chaos of Helen's clothes and put together a few outfits that would work in the cooler Northwest climate, packed toiletries and shoes, and managed to get to the airport in time for our departure. Helen was a pro from all her years of travel, and the excitement of the trip helped her focus long enough to get through security, grab a meal to take on the plane, and board.

Before we took off, Alan had called the kids to let them know Great-Grandma Helen was coming to Seattle. We needed someone to stay with her during the hours we'd be at work. Both Janie and David were happy to pitch in, offering to hang out whenever they had holes in their schedules. Even Mike, my ex, who'd always been close to Papa Paul and Helen, agreed to cover a day. We'd sort out who would do what when we got home, but as we took off from

Oakland we could relax, knowing Helen would be safe with people who loved her.

She seemed to adapt easily, looking around the house and enjoying the company of Janie and David, who stopped by to say hello. Dinner was simple, at home, and quiet. The three of us watched TV before deciding it was time to turn in, showing Helen to her room. We'd put a night light in the bathroom so she could find her way if needed, and kissed her goodnight before heading to our bedroom down the hall.

"Where am I? Why am I here? Help me!" I heard a voice yelling. I nudged Alan, who was not yet asleep.

"It's Helen. I need to go check on her, I think she's confused." I threw on my robe and opened the door. Helen stood outside the bathroom looking completely lost. I walked over and put my arm around her shoulder.

"It's okay, Helen, you're here with us. You're in Seattle, at our home. This is your room here," I said as I guided her back to her bed. "Climb back in and get some sleep. We're right next door."

"But when can I go home? I don't want to stay here. I'm not staying here, am I?" she sounded genuinely frightened. "I want to go back home."

"I know. You're going home in a week. You're not moving up here, I know how much you love San Toro; it's your home. You're just visiting us," I kept reassuring her, keeping my voice calm and soothing. "I know this is a strange house, but you're safe here with us. See if you can get some sleep."

It took almost an hour to get her back into bed and quiet, her fears and confusion requiring all of my patience. Staying relaxed was the only hope I had of keeping Helen from escalating and making things worse. I tried not to look at the clock, knowing I had clients the next day and needed to be fresh and alert.

She finally settled down, exhausted from the events of the day and evening. I tucked her in, just as I had done with Janie and David when they were little and had had nightmares. I tiptoed out of the room, closing the bedroom door gently. I stood in the dimly lit hallway, wondering if bringing Helen to our house had been a good idea. *Hell, no matter what we did she'd be freaking out, so I guess at least this way she's with family and not strangers.* I went back to my room, dropped my robe on the chair by the bed, and climbed in beside Alan.

"How'd it go?" he asked sleepily. "She okay?"

"As good as can be expected," I replied. "As good as can be expected." I kissed him goodnight and rolled over, hoping there wouldn't be a repeat before morning.

The novelty of spending time and going on outings with Mike, Janie, and David entertained Helen during the day. She came home happy to share where they'd been. Mike had taken her to Leavenworth, the quasi-Bavarian tourist town on the eastern side of the Cascades. Janie showed her some of the lovelier horse farms north of Seattle, and David opted for a ferry ride and lunch on one of the local islands. I filled in the gaps with shorter adventures on my free days, and Helen often commented on what a lovely time she was having.

Still, she frequently became agitated about going home. Her persistence in thinking she was being moved permanently to Seattle was upsetting, and I struggled to help her understand she would return to San Toro. It gave me a glimpse into what it must have been like the previous week with the caregivers: the ups and downs, depending on the gaps in Helen's memory. Her anxiety kicked in when she couldn't retain information, and she responded with panic, anger, and accusations. Sitting with her, staying calm, and offering lots of reassurance settled her until the subsequent episode. I wondered if it would ever change, if she would ever find contentment again? Kim had told me those with Alzheimer's ultimately do, but at the moment it was hard to imagine.

Chapter 26

"I am glad we're taking her back to San Toro today, but now I'm worried about the move. How's she going to make sense of all that? They can't tell her she's only there temporarily since she's not." As Alan and I stood in the boarding area awaiting our flight I tried to keep my own anxiety in check, not wanting to give Helen any cause to react. Nearby, Helen chatted with an elderly man seated beside her. At least on this flight the three of us would be sitting together. "God, I hope they're good at this."

We'd plotted out what needed to be accomplished for the move. We'd lined up a local company to handle the larger pieces of furniture and most of her clothes, at least what we'd been able to get packed with all of Helen's interruptions and resistance. We knew we were taking far more than she needed, but hoped having more of her things might offer familiarity and therefore some comfort. She'd be sleeping in her own bed, with her own linens, surrounded by her couch, chair, and love seat from the living room. We'd selected pictures she liked for the walls and a sampling of her travel journals for the bookcase in the spare room. The trundle bed was going, along with various other items Helen had indicated she wanted. The plan was to make the two-bedroom space feel homey and safe.

We'd worked with the management at Duncan House to disconnect the stove, worried that Helen might attempt to cook and forget she had done so. One of my friends who worked as a companion to similar patients explained the concept of therapeutic lying: telling small fibs that serve to calm and reassure, to redirect focus, and to protect. The 'broken' stove, and the follow-up 'we've reported it to maintenance,' was one such white lie. I had no guilt employing this strategy if it helped Helen. She'd be momentarily upset and then just as quickly move on to something else.

The move-in day was remarkably uneventful. Helen participated in decorating decisions, albeit with uneven focus and attention, but seemed pleased with the apartment when we were finished. Alan and I planned to stay over in the spare room to see how the first night went before flying home for the week. After unpacking most of the boxes, we escorted Helen to dinner in the front building, not only to eat, but also to evaluate her ability to find her way once we were gone.

The dining room was tastefully decorated with linens, wine glasses, and menus. Helen had yet to be given a seat assignment, so for the first meal she stayed with us at a row of small tables near a group of women chatting pleasantly. She enjoyed watching all the activity as the staff helped other residents and stopped by our table frequently to see how we were doing.

"Can Bruce come back now? No one can complain that he won't be taken care of here." That had been one of Duncan House's major selling points for Helen. The possibility that they could be reunited had been raised repeatedly during the move and now that she was in the facility her persistence in asking was unrelenting. As we returned to Helen's apartment, I called Myron to broach the subject. I mentioned Helen's willingness to move into a facility and her continued wish to be reunited with Bruce. He was surprisingly open, relaying his father's desire to be with Helen as well. Their connection was far stronger than Myron had realized, and while he preferred having him closer to his house he had to ultimately acquiesce to his father's wishes. Having him at a facility allayed his fears for his care, and we made plans to have him transferred once Helen was settled.

"He's going to come to Duncan House to be with you, probably sometime next week," I said as I hung up the phone. Helen began to cry, but for once they were tears of delight. "Let's get you comfortable so when he does come you can show him around."

The first night went well. Alan guessed Helen was exhausted from the move and relieved she'd soon be seeing Bruce. Whatever the reason, we were glad she seemed to be adapting so easily. We spent the following morning walking her to and from the main building, hoping to create patterns she might remember when on her own, but we soon realized it was too overwhelming.

"Natalie, what options are there to help Helen? I can see her getting totally lost just from her apartment to the dining room. She probably belongs in this building instead of the back one, but it's what it took to get her here in the first place." I was sitting with the resident manager in the lobby. Alan was upstairs, helping Helen unpack one of the remaining boxes.

"A lot of residents hire caregivers for a variety of tasks. Some only come in for short periods, others have them all day. I can give you some names of a few who are here already and may be able to spend some time with Helen. It's less expensive than hiring an agency from outside since those charge travel time and mileage." She excused herself and went to her office, returning a few minutes later with a printed sheet containing several names and phone numbers. "You can probably get hold of a couple of them now who are working today."

I thanked her and went out to the small bench in front of the entrance to make the calls. I got voice mail the first numbers I tried, but reached a woman named Consuela on my third attempt who agreed to meet in the lobby in fifteen minutes. Rather than go back to the apartment and then have to find another excuse to leave, I took the opportunity to make a cup of tea in the library and just sit, enjoying the few moments of silence. I observed residents, staff, and family members coming and going; the atmosphere was as friendly and relaxed as it had been on my first visit. The place felt like a good fit for Helen: nice, but not ostentatious, with enough activity in the main areas to support her need for social interaction.

"Are you Shelly?" A woman approached from one of the side halls. "I'm Consuela. Nice to meet you." Her age was difficult to determine, somewhere between forty and early fifties, and she was dressed in neat khaki pants and a white shirt with her black hair pulled back into a ponytail. Unlike the staff, she had no nametag, but her bearing indicated she was familiar with the facility and definitely wasn't a resident.

"Hi, Consuela. Yes, I'm Shelly. Have a seat and let's chat. I understand you help several residents here. My grandmother moved in last night and we're concerned about her finding her way around, at least at first. She has memory issues but is very stubborn and independent, so hates to have help. I'm sure you've never heard of someone like that before," I added with a laugh. I guessed I was describing many of the elderly adults upon their arrival here, hating to lose their freedom, feeling marginalized, and yet needing assistance.

"Oh yes, I've had my share of clients like that. Thankfully all but a few come around fairly soon and end up liking it here. It's such a change for them to give up their homes, but they do appreciate the care they get. Speaking of care, what are you looking for?"

"I'm not totally sure. I know we need someone to help Helen get to and from meals. She hasn't been able to figure out the way, and I have no idea how long that will take. So that's the start. Is this something you do?" Consuela nodded, and we continued talking about costs, times, and Helen's personality. I felt comfortable with her and asked if she could come up to the apartment to meet Helen. I phoned Alan to warn him.

As expected, Helen wasn't pleased with the decision to hire Consuela, or anyone else, to—as she put it—'take me out for walks.' Once again by employing a couple of small white lies, 'Duncan House likes to use caregivers with many of their new residents until they get comfortable,' and 'it's included in the rent you pay,' I was able to convince Helen she didn't have a choice. She seemed to have a positive first impression of Consuela, but then again, she'd liked Laney and Marie at first, too. This time, however, Consuela would only be around in short bursts, not just helping Helen find her way, but also being my eyes and ears once we left town.

Following lunch we brought Helen back to her room to pick up our bags before leaving for the airport and returning to Seattle. We hoped to get in another full week of work before driving back with our truck to begin the arduous task of clearing out the house in preparation for renters. We reminded Helen of our plans, and that Consuela would be coming by to help her get to dinner. As we stood to leave, Helen hugged us both and walked arm-in-arm with me to the door. One final hug and we left, waving goodbye as we headed down the hall.

"No, don't go, don't leave me!" a wail came from behind as we turned the corner to the elevator. "Don't make me stay here! I can't stay!" Helen ran down the hall, screaming hysterically. She flew into my arms, begging and pleading with me not to leave. It was far worse than the episode at the house; this time she was having a full panic attack.

"Don't warehouse me! Don't leave me here alone!" I was once again struck by how young Helen felt in my arms.

I let her cry, holding her and comforting her. But this time we had to leave; we couldn't bring her to Seattle and we couldn't stay in San Toro. I motioned to Alan to call Consuela, hoping that having someone with her might make our leave-taking slightly less agonizing. She arrived within minutes, and offered to sit with Helen so we could make our flight. Helen resisted, clinging to me, begging us not to go. I felt like crying myself, a mixture of pain and guilt, but Alan stepped in, encouraging Helen to let go, reminding her we'd be back soon and that Consuela would help calm her. His soothing demeanor, which usually worked so well with Helen, failed to stop the flow of tears. He finally pulled her gently away and into the waiting embrace of Consuela. His firmness helped me as well. We had to go at some point and delaying would only mean we'd go through this again later.

"I love you, Helen, we'll be back soon, I promise. You'll be okay here; Consuela will stay with you," my words meant to reassure me as much as Helen. "We have to go now, but we'll be back." I kept repeating myself as we resumed our walk to the elevator.

"Show me your rooms," Consuela said, her arm around Helen's shoulder, as she gently but assertively turned her back toward the apartment. "I didn't get to see everything when I was there earlier," I heard as we turned the corner.

"Oh my God, that was exhausting," Alan commented as we sat in the car, neither of us moving. "I feel like crap leaving her like that."

"Tell me about it. I can only surmise it was like flashback for her, being left as a kid. I felt completely helpless to comfort her."

Alan had heard parts of Helen's story before, how she was placed in a children's home at age seven, along with her siblings, in the midst of the Depression, and her father was forced to work several jobs to support them. Helen attended nursing school in the hopes of helping her older brother Bobby pay for college when World War II ended; his death on his twenty-second birthday from a Kamikaze airstrike had left a scar that still brought tears to her eyes fifty years later.

But some stories Helen only revealed while we were sitting quietly late at night while Papa Paul lay in his hospital bed dying, and those were the ones I chose to share now with Alan. The more I thought about them, the more they helped create a greater context for Helen's current behavior. Helen's father, the one she had depended on and idolized, died of lung cancer when she was only thirteen; as a result of his death, she stayed at the children's home until she graduated high school. As she opened up to me, she confessed to the humiliation she felt, never wanting anyone to think less of her for not being raised by her parents. I disclosed to Alan that Helen's middle sister suffered from, in Helen's words, diminished mental capabilities, another source of embarrassment in those days. The deepest shame came from her mother's suicide, who leaped to her death from a fifth story window while confined to a mental institution, which explained her absence from all of Helen's stories. I'd always wondered why she had never mentioned her before, and after sharing this secret I better understood the reluctance to acknowledge her. Generationally, these were topics one never addressed, instead burying them and believing they could be forgotten. How cruel that the disease robbing her of her memory left her with images she no longer had the capacity to make sense of; all that remained was the ability to continually relive the pain and fear.

"We need to do something so she isn't constantly re-traumatized every time we have to leave." *Or that I'm traumatized every time I leave her.*

Shelly

Chapter 27

I turned my phone back on after Alan and I exited the movie. It was our first date night in several months, courtesy of a free offering through our bank's credit card services, to see a preview of an upcoming theatrical release. The chance to relax and talk about something besides the stress of work or Helen was a most welcome gift. The movie had been entertaining, the popcorn extra buttery, and holding hands in the dark reminded me of when we'd first met.

"How in the world can I have fourteen messages? Who would call me?" I glanced quizzically at my phone. "Even a client emergency wouldn't have that many voicemails; they'd call my back-up." I listened to the first one.

"Hi, Shelly, it's Helen. Please call me. I want my sewing machine; it's not here. I want to be able to sew, I want it brought here right away. Where is it? I am very angry that it's not here. Please call me as soon as you get this message. I want my sewing machine." The message continued in this fashion until it timed out.

"Shelly, it's Helen. Please call me. Where is my sewing machine? I want it now. I need you to bring it to me. Where is it? And I want my sewing box. I may need to repair some of my clothes and I want to have it here. Call me. It's Helen." Again, a full message timed out.

Alan and I had carefully helped Helen pick items to take that would fit comfortably in the space at Duncan House, be of use to Helen, and bring her good memories of her past. The sewing machine, while clearly holding significance, didn't fit any of the criteria. Helen hadn't really cared about it when we were selecting furniture either, thus its being left off the list. I wonder if she'd touched it during the entire time she'd been with Bruce, but now it had assumed an importance beyond all reason.

"Shelly, it's Helen. Where are my blue shoes? Where is the other chair? Where is my sewing machine? I am very angry. I think someone took my things. I think you are keeping my things from me. Where are you? Why aren't you calling me back? It's Helen." Click.

Each call filled the entire allotted time and contained a variation of the same theme: something was stolen, missing, being kept from her. No one was helping her. After the first three messages I simply let them play in the background, fearful I might miss something of importance, but unwilling to devote the time to paying close attention.

Fourteen messages, each one a rambling complaint about missing items, sewing machines, and people stealing. Twenty minutes listening to the pain and agony of a woman who was struggling to make sense of her new world.

"I know I should call her back, but it really is too late tonight, and I don't want to get into a long conversation that just recycles everything. I can't believe there's any benefit in that for Helen; I think it will only get her worked up. I'm going to hope that tomorrow she's forgotten it all."

"She might forget calling, but I doubt she'll be settled." Alan was right; she'd been agitated on some level the entire visit to Seattle. There was no reason to believe she'd become comfortable in her new environment, surrounded by strangers, in only a few days.

His prediction was accurate: the calls continued, and when I picked up the occasional one, Helen agonized about her current issue for what felt like an eternity. It didn't matter what I said, and after the first few calls I learned to simply listen and let her ramble on until she was exhausted. At that point I promised to look into the most egregious of her concerns and take care of things, knowing I wouldn't actually do anything and that Helen wouldn't remember anyway.

"I'm so sick of feeling guilty all the time," I said over drinks with my friend Grace. We hadn't been out since things had unraveled with Helen, and it felt good to catch up. "I feel crappy if I talk to her and she's complaining, and I feel crappy if I let it go to voicemail. I guess I'm resigned to feeling crappy." I reached for my glass of Malbec, swirling it around before taking a sip.

"Sounds like there's no right way to do this," Grace agreed. "Sucks no matter what you do, so you need to take care of yourself. Besides hanging out with me tonight, what are you doing to get some relief? Are you and Alan getting time alone? Is there anyone else who can pitch in? Your mom or your brother?" she asked, although she already knew the answer, having heard my family stories over the years. "Are you okay financially? Will that impact what you can do?"

"Thank God she was so frugal with money, even more so after Papa Paul died. She and Bruce took some trips, but he was financially secure and probably as tight as she was, so no extravagant tours or crazy purchases. Even with this current down market she's in good shape; Bruce's son managed her investments, but apparently she was too absent-minded, or scattered, to follow up on paperwork, so a lot of her money is still in cash. Who'd have thought that was a good idea until now? It frees me to make the best, right decisions for her, to make sure she is cared for the way he'd want her to be and she deserves to be. At least that part isn't making me feel guilty!" I took a long swallow of wine.

"And yes, the reality is there isn't anyone else to help. I don't even know if Gary would do much if he were here; he and Helen had such a contentious relationship." I couldn't remember a time when I'd counted on him for anything, and he'd never volunteered to help in any way.

"I haven't really thought much about him other than filling in the attorney on some Trust details. Once he moved to Japan four years ago there's only been minimal contact." I hadn't missed him because I'd seen him so infrequently prior to his relocation that nothing had really changed. We didn't live near each other, had no shared interests, and even as young children hadn't been particularly close. It wasn't a bad relationship, just a distant one: superficial and friendly when we saw each other, but our lives ran in completely different circles. In the rare times we were all together as a family, he could become antagonistic if the subject touched on anything controversial. I simply stayed away from hot topics when I did see him; it was much simpler that way.

"Talking about him reminds me that I should fill him in on what's going on now that the dust has settled."

"Probably good to let him know what you're doing, unless you think your mom told him. I have to imagine he'll feel some concern, and will appreciate you keeping him in the loop. After that, it's just figuring out how to live with feeling shitty," Grace smiled. "Drinks with best friends are one of the ways!" We clinked our glasses.

"And changing the subject is another! Tell me about your love life. How's the dance scene going?" I laughed, and our talk drifted to the intricacies of online dating, swing dancing, and the frustrations of being single. Grace had been a major support when I'd gone through my divorce years earlier; it was now my turn to be there for her, and, selfishly, it felt good to be talking about something besides dementia, caregivers, and family.

Chapter 28

To: Gary.Wylings@qusmail.japan
From: ShellyJ.123@qusmail.usa
Subject: Helen's health

Hi Gary,

Hope you're doing well. I can't really imagine living in Japan, but I know you've always been fascinated by the culture and language. Glad it's been a good fit for you!

I'm not sure if Mom told you what's been going on here the last few weeks with Helen, but thought I'd catch you up in any case. Helen was diagnosed with Alzheimer's and the doctors said she could no longer live alone. She and I checked out several places and settled on Duncan House, a facility that can help manage some of the concerns her illness raised. She struggles with short-term memory, like remembering to cook. She's starting to get settled. I don't know if you ever met Bruce, her partner, but he's going to be moving in with her soon.

Things came about quite suddenly and it's been pretty crazy until now. I'm finally catching my breath and finding the bandwidth to reconnect with the rest of the world. I had to do a lot of quick planning and decision making, so sorry I didn't email you myself. There's not much you can do from over there.

On another note, I've been cleaning out the house to get it ready to lease and wanted to know if there is anything you'd like. Anything of sentimental value of Papa Paul's? Most of their stuff will be donated to charity since the value is

177

low, but if there is something special you want, let me know.

I've included Helen's new address at the end of this so you can contact her. I know she'd enjoy getting mail.

I'll keep you posted as things unfold or if anything requires a decision from you. I apologize for not getting to you sooner.

Ciao,
Shelly

Alan and I had talked briefly about what to say, not overly concerned with Gary's reaction since he had never been close to Helen. I felt bad that I'd waited so long, but Alan reminded me of the chaos we'd been living with for the past weeks.

"Honestly, Shelly, the reality is it never even came up, and anyway, how could he have helped? He certainly wasn't going to fly back to San Toro for this."

I knew he was right, but it still felt weird to have had so much happen and not even think of him. But the truth was I hadn't.

To: ShellyJ.123@qusmail.usa
From: Gary.Wylings@qusmail.japan
Subject: Re: Helen

Your email came as quite a surprise. I remember Helen as a vibrant woman, capable of taking care of anything put in her way. How did this happen? How are you paying for her care? Is where she's staying the best place for her? What about leaving her at home?

I'd really like to be kept informed from now on.

Gary

"He took that rather well," I said after I read Alan Gary's email. "Reduces my guilt somewhat. I'll shoot him another note to answer his questions. I'm sure it'll put his mind to ease knowing we don't have to sweat the cost of her care."

I composed a straightforward letter outlining Helen's decision for me to work with a financial planner to oversee her accounts. I described the doctor's impressions, our tours to the various facilities, and let him know I intended to keep him up to date as I made decisions about the house. It felt better to be including him in what I was doing, even though there wasn't much for him to contribute. My role was clearly defined by the law, and the responsibility was on me, but it was nice to think he'd be supporting me from afar.

My relief was short-lived, however, when I awoke the next morning and read my email.

To: ShellyJ.123@qusmail.usa
From: Gary.Wylings@ qusmail.usa
Subject: Re: Helen

I am furious you didn't contact me directly when all this happened. As the oldest in the family, I have a right to know what is going on and I expect to be fully consulted on all matters. You cannot handle this on your own, and I expect to be consulted regarding every decision concerning the house and finances. How can I be sure you aren't wasting money and making poor choices? You can't do anything without my input from now on.
Gary

To: Gary.Wylings@ qusmail.usa
From: ShellyJ.123@qusmail.usa
Subject: re: Helen

I just said I intended to keep you in the loop regarding major decisions, but I don't plan to run every little detail by you. Besides being onerous and time consuming, it's not how the Trust was set up. Papa Paul and Helen made their choice as to who to put in charge, and I can only honor what they did.
Shelly

"I actually understand his initial anger at not being informed directly by me, but it's not like we ever talk about anything anyway.

The annual Christmas card, with a brief 'life's great here' and his name's all it's been for years. Here I am trying to involve him, he starts off being gracious, now he's starting to question every decision," I told Alan as we walked through our neighborhood one afternoon. He'd sent three more emails, all making demands, within hours of his previous one. "Do I keep explaining my position as Trustee to him? That I'm the one in charge of her care and that's what she wants as well?"

"Is this what he was like with your grandparents? What caused the friction with them?" Alan had only met Gary briefly; he'd moved to Japan not long after Alan and I married.

"I remember him as stubborn and opinionated, tossing in odd comments just to see if he could get a rise out of everyone, but it was mostly harmless. He went through phases of not coming to San Toro for family events, then attending but arriving late or leaving early. His anger was primarily directed at our mom. It'd be quiet for a while, but it was always simmering below the surface. To be sure, she wasn't a great parent, but at what point do you simply move on? Doesn't there come a time to let go of childhood baggage?"

I thought back on the role I'd played in the family dynamics, trying to mediate the friction between my grandparents, my mother, and brother. I'd explain to the adults that my brother had had some tough breaks and made some poor choices, but that he had finally made his way, that he was now independently supporting himself and had found a career path he seemed to like. I'd then turn to my brother and try to help him understand that the older members of the family simply cared and wanted to see him be responsible and successful; that they were a product of a different generation and had different ways of handling things. Tempers would calm down, relationships would improve for a while, and I would once again hope that everything was resolved.

"You really think he'll hear you? Think he'll actually change as a result of anything you say?" Alan was probably right, but my nature was to keep trying.

"I can't help but think I need to give him more information, make sure he feels included, and some time to digest it all. It's got to be hard feeling left out of any role in the Trust."

"Go ahead if it'll make you feel better," Alan shrugged.

To: Gary.Wylings@qusmail.japan
From: ShellyJ.123@qusmail.usa
Subject: re: Helen

I'm not going to break down every choice Helen and I made, nor the details of all the costs involved. You're entitled to an annual report regarding expenses and income, but including you in every decision isn't reasonable, especially with you far away. I'm trying my best to keep you informed as to what I'm doing. I get it that you can't see what's going on here, but that's the reality we're in. I want your support since I am the one dealing with everything and I want you to trust that I am doing my best not only in regards Helen but to the financial decisions as well.

Shelly

To: ShellyJ.123@qusmail.usa
From: Gary.Wylings@qusmail.japan
Subject: Re: Helen

What is it costing to keep her there? What do they provide that can't be done at home? I think it's a waste of her money to pay for where she is. And I want to know how it got this bad? If you're so close to her, why didn't you see it sooner? And whatever you do, don't sell the house. I'm very worried about the choices you're making.

Gary

"WTF?" I stared at the email. "Alan, come check this out. He's second-guessing everything I'm doing. He isn't even here to understand her condition or her situation."

"Back-seat driving, huh? Doesn't want to come out and see for himself, but wants to tell you how to handle things. Nice."

"So what do I do? Keep giving him information? How much is enough; when is it enough?" I could feel myself getting angry at Gary's insinuation that I was doing things wrong.

"Let's just sit on it for a while. No need to respond right away, and it'll give you a chance to calm down." Alan's suggestion to table further discussion was a good one, although I still felt the urge to explain myself.

Later, when we'd finished dinner and were sitting on the couch, I asked Alan, "What is it with my family that they hook me so quickly?" It was our evening ritual, to put everything aside and sit together, discussing the events of our day, things we were interested in or had heard or read about, or simply being quiet in the same space. There hadn't been time for it most days the past few weeks, and it felt good to be back into the regular routine. I'd been able to get in a nice, long run in the morning and seeing clients the rest of the day had been a good diversion. I felt calmer and more focused. But it was still frustrating to re-read Gary's latest email.

"I get it that he must feel something being the older brother and bypassed by our grandparents, but it's nothing new. He's definitely known I'd be in charge since Papa Paul died and he never said anything then. He's got to know I didn't ask for this, I was just closer to Helen. Besides, he's not even here, offering opinions without any information." I could feel the tension starting to rise, and along with it the familiar twinge of guilt. *I* had been the favored grandchild; *he* had been shunned from the time he was a teen because of his poor choices and contrarian attitude. But I was also the one who'd maintained close ties to my grandparents; he was the one who chose to move half a world away. In all my talks with Helen over the years he was rarely mentioned. Redefining his role, or lack thereof, as it pertained to the Trust or her care had never been discussed in any of Helen's estate planning.

"He's being an ass and I still feel guilty," I stopped, taking a few deep breaths before continuing. "Okay, I need to focus on my response, not that stuff."

Alan listened patiently. I knew he'd offer some good insights when I finished, and that he was only waiting for me to vent before sharing them.

"I think the simpler you make things the better: keep it clean, a lot less confusing. Write separate threads for each issue: Helen's health, the house, and the financial piece. It'll also help clarify where the real conflicts are and what he cares about. Keep explanations to a minimum unless you see he's actually interested in what you think."

As always, his advice was sound and he didn't have the emotional landmines my family could still trigger in me despite years of distance, therapy, and conversations with friends. At least now I could see the patterns and the hooks. In the past I simply reacted and regretted it later.

We spent the next half hour wording answers to his email and accusations, careful to acknowledge some of his concerns without conceding to his demands.

To: Gary.Wylings@qusmail.japan
From: ShellyJ.123@qusmail.usa
Subject: Helen's heath

I understand your frustration with only finding out now about Helen's decline. It was a shock to me as well since it's hard to notice from a distance. It was only when I stayed with her that I really understood what was going on, and

I'm sorry I was unable to inform you earlier. You have no idea how crazy it was between meetings with all the doctors, social workers, facilities, and moving. It's all been a blur.

I'd like to suggest you read up on Alzheimer's so you understand what's happening with Helen. It's really tragic to see her struggles with memory, and it's quite an insidious disease. It often takes a long time to recognize that subtle changes aren't simply normal aging, and it's even harder when living far apart. From some of what I've read it may have been going on for years without any symptoms, but her car accident a year ago and resulting loss of independence and social connections most likely precipitated the more recent, and rapid, decline.

The prognosis is a gradual decrease in functioning, though it's reasonable to expect her to live for many more years unless some other illness occurs first. My intent is to care for her the way she and Papa Paul would want; it's what they saved for.

I'll keep you informed of any major changes in status. Again, I've attached the address for Duncan House so you can send her cards if you'd like. I'm sure she'd like to receive mail.

Shelly

"One down, two more to go," I pushed away from the desk while Alan leaned in to read my words.

"Looks good," he said, returning to the chair he'd been occupying in the corner of our shared home office. I clicked 'send.'

"Now for the house. This one should be easier." My fingers moved across the keyboard.

To: Gary.Wylings@qusmail.japan
From: ShellyJ.123@qusmail.usa
Subject: Helen's house

As I mentioned earlier, I'm going to lease the house for the time being. It'll give Helen a chance to adjust to her new circumstances without having to deal with losing her home. The realtor we're using has gone over the property with me and I'm following his suggestions as to what to do to prepare it for rental. It should go on the market in the next week or two.

The house has been emptied of the major items. I have a few boxes of things that belonged to Papa Paul that might hold sentimental value for you, so please let me know if there's anything you might want before I donate what's left.

Shelly

I read it aloud. Alan simply smiled his approval.

"Okay, last one," I murmured. "The hardest to talk about, but probably the most important of the three." I began composing the one regarding the Trust, which I knew was really about our grandparents' money and probably, on an even deeper level, feeling valued by them. I started and stopped several times, re-wording it with Alan's help before arriving at the message I wanted to convey.

To: Gary.Wylings@qusmail.japan
From: ShellyJ.123@qusmail.usa
Subject: Trust and finances

As I said before, it was Helen and Papa Paul's choice to put whomever they wanted in charge. I'm sorry if that disappoints you, but it was their decision to make, not ours.

As Trustee, one of my primary roles is to make sure Helen is taken care of financially. As she wished, I will make all decisions in consultation with the financial planner she and I chose together.

Shelly

I was glad we'd spent the time composing the emails before we went to bed. I knew it would have rattled about in my mind all night and it felt better to get them sent. I doubted Gary would calm down, but it was still important for me to keep communicating with him.

Chapter 29

To: ShellyJ.123@qusmail.usa
From: Gary.Wylings@qusmail.japan
Re: Trust and finances

I don't care how stressed you were. I should have been involved in all of your talks with the social workers, lawyers, and financial planners. As the oldest my input should have been considered.

I don't understand why you even have a financial planner. They just rip you off. If you lose money, it will be your fault, and I will do everything I can to hold you responsible.

Gary

"Well, that wasn't the positive response I was hoping for," I said sarcastically as I passed my laptop over to Alan to read Gary's email. "Not what I was expecting to read first thing this morning."

I walked into the kitchen and opened the cabinet to get the bowls for cereal while Alan read the note. I slid out the utensil drawer, grabbed spoons, and shoved it closed with my hip. Returning to the table, I placed the items on our respective place mats before going back for the Raisin Bran and milk.

"Thoughts? Reactions?" I inquired as Alan pushed the laptop away.

I sat down next to him and unfolded the top of the cereal box. Shaking out a small portion, I handed it to Alan before adding milk to my bowl. I took a bite, trying to be patient while Alan formulated his response.

At times I loved his deliberative process; at others, I found myself tapping my feet, urging him to speak up. I had learned, however, in the years we'd been married, that as frustrating as it could be, his calmness was a good balance to my tendency to overreact. In turn, he appreciated my insights and perspectives, my way of viewing things from an emotional center. We made a good team.

"I don't see any questions in his response, only his same demands. You don't necessarily have to answer him, since there's nothing new to actually reply to," he said as he poured his cereal. "I know you'll want to do something because I know how hard it is for you to just let it go, but let's sit on it for now."

"But…" I started before shutting my mouth. Reluctantly I had to agree. "You're right; my first instinct is to defend myself and there's no point in that. The attorney said it's best to keep him informed, but I'm not sure how far that goes. Given how he's behaving, I definitely don't want his advice."

I took a spoonful of my breakfast before continuing. "I want to respond, but I also want to be careful I don't open any doors. If this is how he's going to react I have no intention of listening to any of his opinions. No help from people who understand money management? Is he serious?"

Later that morning Alan and I composed a short message to acknowledge Gary's email without eliciting his help. Maybe he just needed more clarification.

To: Gary.Wylings@qusmail.japan
From: ShellyJ.123@qusmail.usa
Re: Trust and finances

Gary,

To reiterate, Helen and I selected a financial planner we both trust who will help me make decisions that balance Helen's needs for income and preserve her assets. This is part of my legal duty as Fiduciary.

Shelly

To: ShellyJ.123@qusmail.usa
From: Gary.Wylings@qusmail.japan
Re: Trust and finances

Financial people are bloodsuckers just trying to get your money. If you don't think you can manage the Trust I'm happy to take it over. I've been reading and studying articles and have a good handle on what should be done. At the very least I expect you to ask my opinion on any decisions you make with the planners. I'm warning you: it will be on your head if you lose any money.

Gary

This time I opted to ignore his email. Alan was right: there was no question, thus no need to reply. His urgency and demanding tone wasn't moderating. If anything it was getting worse. Best to disengage and see if he mellowed over time, although by now I had doubts that would happen. He'd already forwarded a dozen articles predicting doom, gloom, and his ideas of where I should put the Trust money, all of which I moved to the computer trash bin. Better to stick to less controversial subjects, keeping the lines of dialogue open as recommended by the attorney. His theory was the better the relationships within the family, the fewer legal fights later. I certainly wanted that to be the case, although given our family it was fifty-fifty at best.

To: Gary.Wylings@qusmail.japan
From: ShellyJ.123@qusmail.usa
Subject: Helen's health update

Helen's had some panic attacks. The staff here said this is quite common when dementia patients are moved out of their homes and typically subsides over time.

I've brought in a care team consisting of a doctor and a psychiatrist, and we're working to get her stabilized, using a combination of medications and caregivers to help her adjust to her new environment. We're definitely seeing progress, but it's been stressful for her. Bruce has also moved back to be with her and that has certainly helped. Just wanted to keep you updated.

Shelly

To: ShellyJ.123@qusmail.usa
From: Gary.Wylings@qusmail.japan
Re: Helen's health update

Is Bruce living off of Helen? Who is paying for his care? You better not be supporting him. In any case you should have left her in the house and had Mom come and live with her. They'd be able to take care of each other and it'd save money for both of them. Her decline is unconscionable.

Gary

I was speechless. I slammed down the lid of my laptop, resisting the urge to throw it across the room. I'd been trying to keep him updated and all he did was continue to attack me almost constantly via emails. No matter what I wrote he challenged me, demanding I concede to his wishes. I hadn't answered most of them; instead, filing them in a folder in case I needed a reminder later of how he had treated me. My hopes for keeping a civil relationship were rapidly dwindling, and it was time to change the dynamics. I was done listening to him.

To: Gary.Wylings@qusmail.japan
From: ShellyJ.123@qusmail.usa
Re: Helen's health update

Are you serious? Do you have any idea what it would be like for Mom and Helen to be in the same house for a few days, let alone permanently? They'd kill each other. Besides, Mom is almost 80 and if you recall she had a minor stroke years ago. There's no way she could live in a house with stairs or provide the kind of care Helen's going to need. Not to mention she has a life elsewhere with Julia and wouldn't necessarily want to move.

The reality is Helen needs to be in a care facility that can deal with her Alzheimer's as it progresses. Did you get the book I suggested? It talks about that in detail. Moving her now allows her to make connections and feel safe as her memory deteriorates.

Of course Bruce is paying for his own care, and his living there is very important for Helen's well being. While she is having a hard time now, it's not unusual or unexpected. The consensus of all her caregivers is that she'll mellow over time and be happier around others at Duncan House.

Shelly

To: ShellyJ.123@qusmail.usa
From: Gary.Wylings@qusmail.japan
Re: Helen's health update

I'm sorry. It must be hard for you dealing with all of this. I am so far away I feel helpless. Thanks for the update.

Gary

To: Gary.Wylings@qusmail.japan
From: ShellyJ.123@qusmail.usa
Re: Helen's health update

No problem. I understand you feel disconnected. I'm asking you to trust me and let me do my job here. What I need from you is support.

Shelly

I felt a rush of relief; Gary was calming down. Maybe he was finally beginning to understand that I wasn't trying to exclude him.

To: ShellyJ.123@qusmail.usa
From: Gary.Wylings@qusmail.japan
Re: Helen's health update

I still can't believe you let her get like this. You should've known things were deteriorating and stepped in sooner. You're now throwing away their precious savings to pay others to care for her, and Bruce better not be benefitting from any of her money. You should've consulted me before making all these decisions.

I'm holding you entirely accountable for all the financial decisions you're making. Shame on you for letting things get so out of hand. Papa Paul would be rolling in his grave if he knew you put Helen into an old person's institution instead of keeping her at home and wasting the money he saved for his heirs. I'm just glad he isn't alive to see what you've done.

Gary

I brought my laptop to the breakfast table and opened it to show Alan the latest attack. "It's been barely a day since his conciliatory email, and now look. I actually got suckered into believing he would support me for a change, but this blaming crap's only getting worse. I can't trust his nicer emails since they're followed by ten more like this." I was tired of waking to these missives. I'd had enough. "I'm done. I'm not talking to him any more unless he gets it and stops judging me. I've been giving him the benefit of the doubt, letting him have some time to process all of this, but he's digging in deeper. It's also becoming crystal clear this is really about Helen's money, not her. What is his problem?"

"I'm certainly sick of his emails dominating all our conversations," Alan concurred. "It's one thing when we're dealing with the chaos associated with Helen—she's the innocent in all of this—but he's supposedly a functioning adult who's been given numerous chances to soften his tone. What do you want to do?"

"Call James and get his recommendation. I want it to stop, and he'll know what to say. I can't just tell him to fuck off, but there must be something I can do." Creating a plan always helped.

To: Gary.Wylings@qusmail.japan
From: ShellyJ.123@qusmail.usa
Re: Helen's health update

How dare you accuse me of causing any of Helen's health issues or mismanaging her money. I'm sorry that you may feel left out, but you have no right to treat me like this. Shame on you for your judgments from afar!

If you want to contact me again, start with an apology. Because you've attacked me so viciously, and on the advice of my attorney, I am insisting you send it through him so I don't have to read any more of your venom. His name is James Montgomery and his address is attached. Until then I will block your emails.

Shelly

"Wow, even with the time change it only took a few hours for him to ignore what I sent." I was on the phone with Alan, laptop open to a reply email from Gary. "I haven't looked at it. It's tempting to see what he wrote, but I want to stick to my promise to block him unless he apologizes through James. Am I doing the right thing?"

"You are. If he can't honor even a simple request, and the advice of your attorney, what makes you think things will be any different going forward?" He was, as always, the voice of reason. "It's up to you, but I'm with you on this one."

"Okay, I deleted it; it'll help to not see it. Now to block his email," I said as I walked through the steps. "Done and done. I seriously doubt he'll apologize, but one can hope. Thanks for supporting me. Seems silly to have to call you."

"Not silly. This is painful stuff. I wish I could fix it for you, but we've both dealt with people like this and we both know how it unfolds. You've got to set the boundaries." He was right and I knew it. "Okay, gotta get back to work. Maybe we can start focusing on me leaving here since Helen's become more settled. I'm definitely ready to make a move."

Chapter 30

Life slowly returned to normal. Alan was back at work, and I was seeing clients again on a regular basis. Trips to San Toro had reduced to monthly, weekend visits. The house was leased to a lovely family on a long-term work assignment in the Bay Area and Molly had agreed to keep an eye on it to let us know if anything aroused suspicions. Helen was settling into Duncan House with the help of Bruce's company, the assistance of Consuela as needed, and modern pharmaceuticals. I wasn't thrilled with the idea of medications, but the combination of Helen's unresolved traumas and loss of memory contributing to her normal tendency to become anxious and depressed made it virtually impossible for her to be calm otherwise. At least now she was venturing out of her apartment with Bruce.

His return had been a godsend. After Myron brought him back, it was touching to watch the two of them, and clear that Bruce had missed Helen as much as she had him. She fussed over him, wanting to help with everything, whether he needed her assistance or not. He talked about his 'sweet Helen' and patted the seat next to him for her to come and be with him. She beamed with delight, and her calls became less and less frequent. Consuela reported that the two of them spent time in the main building after meals, chatting with other residents and making friends. I hoped it would continue, but the reality of Bruce's age and declining health was always in the back of my mind. How much longer would he live, and what would happen when he passed? I shuddered thinking about it.

All would have been perfect if not for the continuing flood of emails from my brother. While no longer coming directly to me, I asked James to forward a sampling of them when they arrived. I wanted to keep a pulse on his reactions to see if they would abate over time. Gary sent links to articles about the economy and money management, and kept up his demands to be in charge of the Trust. James initially responded to a few, hoping a new, professional voice would calm him, but Gary simply directed a portion of his anger at the lawyer. Had he changed that much over time, or was this the same person our grandparents had dealt with over the years and I'd been too blind to see? Had this been why they'd skipped over him and put me in charge?

The firewall of the attorney helped, and had reduced his intrusions to more like a gnat buzzing constantly in the background. It freed Alan and me to move on to other matters. "Maybe it's time to deal with your work situation," I mentioned to him one evening in kitchen while we cleaned up from dinner. "We've been tabling it, but it's not going away. I hate to admit it, but I'm terrified of you suddenly not having an income on top of spending money for school."

We'd talked on and off about Alan starting his own business. His passion was still computers, but after years in software development working for large companies he wanted to move into the emerging field of digital forensics. But to make the transition required six months of fulltime coursework, plus the time to grow a referral network and generate business, and the timing had never seemed right. I kept hoping there was a way he could keep his job while managing everything else, but I knew the amount of energy that would take. And even if it were possible I didn't want work to consume our entire lives.

He stood quietly for several minutes before answering. "I'd quit tomorrow if you were okay with it. I'm not afraid of figuring out how we'll manage. I've always landed on my feet and I assume I always will. You're the one who's more cautious and practical. I know it frightens you to have me just walk away from health insurance and a steady paycheck."

"If we were in our thirties I don't think I'd hesitate…well, maybe I'd still hesitate, but I'd feel more confident that you'd have time to get your business started or re-coup our savings if for some reason it didn't work out. When you were younger it was easy to find another job. But I think you're going to face too much age discrimination now, especially in this economy. You're too senior, expensive, and gray-haired. Companies can probably hire two younger people fresh out of college for what you get paid. They wouldn't have your expertise, but no one seems to care about that anymore. And yes, health insurance is terrifying for me, having seen what it's like in my work for those without it who have to pay out of pocket."

"What would it take for you to be comfortable? Yes, it's an option for me to gut it out, but we both know I've been miserable in corporate America for ages. I want to be out on my own and rediscover my passion for my work." His voice was full of reason and calm. "How can we find a way to make it okay for me to quit? We've been putting the tuition money aside for ages; we have almost all of it covered by now."

"I don't know. I only know I feel extremely anxious when it comes up, and I have to figure out how to face that fear. You know I'm not into status or things, but it does scare me to think of losing everything, to lose the house and have nowhere to live. You'd be okay living in a tent, but I'm not so sure I'd be. With all the moving and chaos of my growing up I like stability and a sense of place," I answered honestly. "I need to sit with it a while longer and understand what's keeping me so stuck. But I hate you having to go to work everyday just to appease my paranoia."

"Well, we can always move onto the farm back in Ohio. We could live in the camper and you can grow our food and learn to can vegetables. You'd be so cute as a farmer's wife in a little apron," Alan laughed.

"I don't can," I reminded him.

"I'm sure Christy or Pam would love to teach you," he smiled, offering the expertise of his sisters, both of whom loved preserving fresh fruits and other farm goods.

"I don't think you heard me correctly: I don't can, not 'I don't know how to can'," I clarified. "I have no desire to learn!" I smiled. "I don't even like cooking all that much, I doubt I'll suddenly become Susie Homemaker."

Alan knew very well I wasn't the domestic type. It was actually one of the things he loved most about me: I preferred getting out and doing things to cooking and cleaning. When we were first together he was thrilled we didn't have to spend the entire day making sure the house was perfect before friends came over. "They're coming to see us, not my house," I'd said. "It's clean, it's sanitary; I'm not trying to impress anyone." He readily agreed; another major difference between his first marriage and ours. The list was quite long, and heavily tilted in my favor.

"Let me work on it for awhile. I know I can figure it out if I give it some time." I came back to the topic at hand. "I have to get my head wrapped around a new vision, and I'm not sure what that vision is yet. If I can do that I think I'll be okay."

"I can't ask for more than that," he agreed. "I appreciate your willingness to even go that far. It's scary for me, too; not sure if that helps or makes it worse, but I want you to know I'm not being cavalier about all of this. I just know I don't want to go on as it is right now much longer."

We finished the dishes and headed upstairs to watch a movie. We'd agreed earlier to avoid reading email after dinner; while there weren't any messages from Gary there was always the risk of one being forwarded by James, and neither of us felt any urgency to surf the Internet or read up on the world news. There were enough things to worry about in our own lives; we didn't need to compound them before trying to sleep.

Chapter 31

"What happens when you think about Alan leaving his job? Where do you notice it?" Grace's gentle manner belied her insistence that I face my fear. "What does your head tell you versus what your gut is saying?"

"Damn, we've been friends too long. You've learned all my techniques and now you're turning them on me!" I chuckled. "You'd make a good therapist, you know."

"Don't try and weasel out of this. Answer my question," she insisted.

I took a long sip of my tea, tuning in to my body as the liquid warmed me. We were taking advantage of one of the few clear, crisp sunny days to walk outside, and in the stillness of the air I allowed a stillness to take hold inside me. As we padded along the soft dirt of the trail behind Grace's condo, I focused my attention on the sensations of my movements. I slowed my breathing and felt my mind quieting. I experienced a connection to my anxiety, but this time I was noticing it rather than being driven by it.

"It's all just fear; irrational and controlling fear when I'm able to detach from it enough to see it," I said after several minutes of silence. "I don't want to live in fear, and that's what I've been doing." I took a deep breath. "I want to live freely, to believe in Alan and me, to believe we'll figure it out somehow."

Grace let me meander without interruption. "I want to support him in taking care of himself, and I've sucked at that lately. I've been so focused on my needs and fears, and that's not who I am, or at least, who I want to be." I felt something shifting as I spoke, a calm replacing the knot that had been in my stomach for most of the fall. "I've got to let Alan do what he needs to do and not stay in hell because of me; if I can let this go then it's really only about figuring out a plan to make it happen. Wow, I didn't expect that to be what showed up!" I concluded, turning to look at Grace.

"Neither did I, nor so quickly. Either I'm an amazing therapist or you were on the verge of letting it go anyway," Grace replied. "You've hit on something pretty deep. Where do you think that fear comes from?"

"My mom pops into my head," I said without thinking. "She operates out of fear as well. I think a lot of her manipulative behavior is centered around quelling her anxieties. If she can control her situation she can avoid her own discomfort, and in this case I think I'm doing the same thing."

"That's great, but what are you going to do with it? It's one thing to figure things out, quite another to take action."

"Agreed. But this feels pretty big. The thought of making Alan stay feels horrid; by contrast, his leaving suddenly feels right, not scary. I've been so consumed by my own crap that I've been giving lip service to him quitting, but secretly I've been strategizing ways for him to tolerate staying. God, I hate admitting that." I stopped and stared at Grace. "It's horrible to see that in myself; how'd you get me to speak it out loud?"

"I'm going to go with me being such a great friend and leave it at that. You can buy me lunch as payment," Grace laughed to lighten the mood. "We've both shared a fair number of our dark demons with one another. You know a lot of my dirt, too, dearie."

"Yeah, I suppose I could take it in trade for all the drama I've had to listen to you babble on about," I teased. "Nah, you get lunch for this one. It feels huge."

While this was a monumental shift in my thinking, I knew it was in the right direction. It was hard to see the similarities with my mother, to realize that in trying to keep my own demons at bay, I'd been as devious as I perceived her to be. I'd prided myself on being better than her, more self-aware and honest, yet maybe I wasn't so different after all.

I drove home, eager to share my revelations with Alan. I'd debated calling him, but opted to wait until we could talk in person. Despite my embarrassment at uncovering my less desirable aspects of myself, I felt the urge to share them with him, to let him see all of me. Every time we opened up more to each other I was surprised to find it brought us closer, rather than the judgments I worried would tear us apart.

Besides, I wanted to see his reaction to my willingness to upend our comfortable life, to help him create his exit strategy. Once I made up my mind about something I wanted to get moving as soon as possible. It was frustrating to wait; I was already on to the next stage and the details of getting there became a nuisance.

"So do I owe Grace a meal, too? That was one cheap therapy session!" Alan's pleasure in my change of heart was obvious. "I don't know what caused you to suddenly feel okay with all of this, but I am extremely grateful. Just the knowledge that I'll be getting out of there has already lifted my spirits," he mused. "Now we need to make a roadmap that we can both live with. Much as I'd like to, I can't simply tell them to fuck off on Monday, but we have to move swiftly before it becomes obvious I'm more checked out than I already am. If I can fake it till the fall I can start the program then. The timing would be perfect."

"Seems reasonable…gives us several months to get organized. I wish for both our sakes it could be sooner, though," I concurred.

We spent the remainder of the afternoon reviewing our finances and exploring where we could make meaningful cuts in the budget. My additional financial contribution would be to increase my caseload by opening up a few more hours to see clients. He'd start making the arrangements necessary to enroll in school and organize the payment plan. We were beginning to make things happen.

Chapter 32

"I have been thinking a lot about my motives. Helen's situation has brought up a lot of family crap that's been on the back burner for years," I said to Alan one evening over a candlelit dinner in the great room. Since our belt-tightening conversations we'd opted to make meals at home and drink some of the wine we'd collected over the past few years instead of going to the local bistro for a date night.

"My grandparents took pride in how frugal they were and I've tried to model myself after them. On the other side is my mother: spend, keep spending, and then ask someone to bail her out. Reading some of those letters between Papa Paul and her opened my eyes to how deeply rooted she is in abdicating responsibility and playing the victim."

I took a bite of salad, chewing while I pondered the differences between my mother and me. I had been noticing a growing sense of righteousness as I thought of depriving myself of unneeded luxuries in order to pinch pennies and grow our nest egg. The idea of being noble was appealing; I liked being the 'good one' in the family, the one who was practical and could see the bigger picture and make the correct choices.

"I hate admitting, even to you, that I can get pretty smug when I look at my mom and compare most of our decisions. I definitely disagree with many she makes, and I'm okay with that. But somehow I have given myself credit for being better than her, making better choices. Sure, many of my choices have been better, but the underlying motives, and even the execution, are often the same. I think some of it is modeled behavior, like asking indirectly for what I want rather than coming straight out. That doesn't sit well." I took another bite of food, suddenly afraid to look at Alan.

I felt a small flutter of shame as I voiced my deepest negative thoughts, but I realized it was balanced by a sense of relief. If I could speak them, I could do something about them. "It's funny when I compare my reaction to my mom and my reaction to Helen. They both had crappy childhoods: Helen had tons of trauma, my mom's parents divorced and her stepfather was an alcoholic; but I have more compassion for Helen's story. Is it the content or is it how they express it?" I took a sip of my wine, letting the liquid slowly swirl in my mouth before swallowing.

"I think it's less about the actual events than about how they deal with it. I can't remember Helen ever using her past as an excuse for her behavior; instead, it's almost the opposite. She works to prove her worth on her own merits, wants to make sure others are taken care of, and shares the good memories of travel and adventure. My mother, on the other hand, uses her stories to induce guilt. She makes everyone else feel bad for her, gets them to help her, at least until she burns them out, then looks for someone new. Tons of people have crappy childhoods, but it's ridiculous to use it to garner sympathy."

I paused. "Overall, I'm more like Helen, trying to use my experiences to help others, and working hard to focus on the positive stuff; maybe that's why I feel closer to her and why my mom pisses me off so much."

"I think we all have mixed reasons for doing what we do," Alan offered.

"Of course," I countered. "But I still want to pay attention to what's driving my actions. If it's fear then I need to confront the fear rather than manipulate others into doing things to mitigate it. If it ticks me off that my mom can't look at her own behavior, then I certainly better be looking at mine."

"True, and while I think you're probably being too self-critical, I appreciate your ability to look at yourself, and I value it, at least most of the time, when you challenge me to do the same. I think we've both grown as a result, and it's one of the things I like about you," he smiled at me. I felt the truth in his words, and once again marveled at my luck in winning the lottery when I met him.

"I can see where sometimes you ask me questions in such a way that it feels like you want a certain answer rather than being open-ended," he continued. "I figure it's when you're worried about something.

"I'm pretty comfortable holding my own, but I'm not sure everyone is, so I see your point."

"So keep calling me out on it if I miss it. Gives me a chance to do something about it, and keeps me from seeing myself as the good one, from becoming too smug."

"Ah, so it's okay to be a little smug as long as it's only a tiny bit, and that the greater motives are the 'right ones' then?" Alan laughed. This time I joined him, picking up my glass and clinking it against his.

"Exactly! A certain smugness is good," I smiled. "Realistically, talking about it helps, and keeps me in check. What drives me nuts is that my mom's always justifying her positions, always looking for excuses and something to blame: the planets aren't aligned right, a 'sudden expense' occurred despite having the same 'sudden expense' occur every year at the same time; whatever it is, she can't own any responsibility for it. Growing up I always dreaded being anything like her, and I went so far the other way that I became equally stuck in being hyper responsible. Same coin, different sides, but mine's more socially acceptable."

"Makes sense," Alan concurred. "Probably why we get along as well. When something comes up we've both been willing to tackle it head on, without excuses, even when it's tough. I definitely don't see your mom doing that, and we're not going to change her. But enough heady talk for one night; my limit for deep introspection has been maxed out. Let's go upstairs and watch something; I think *Office Space* is on soon."

Chapter 33

"Hi Mom. How're you doing? Thought I'd update you on Helen, and on us." I kept my voice light despite the knot in my stomach that showed up every time I called.

"I'm good. I had a couple of really angry letters from Gary, and I wrote him back letting him have it. I can't for the life of me understand where he gets his crazy notions. He's obsessed with money and wants you ousted. Where's he getting these ridiculous ideas? I think it's the drugs he took; they messed up his brain." I knew better than to comment on my mother's attributions. The temptation to react with, 'Well, gee, Mom, I wonder,' was always on the tip of my tongue but trying to argue the point was useless.

"Or it was that therapist we sent him to in high school who blamed everything on mothers, and ever since then Gary has focused his anger at me," she went on. I chuckled at the fact she blamed everything on her own parents, but commenting about that detail would also be a waste of energy. Placating was a more productive strategy for moving the conversation forward.

"I know, Mom. That was the trend in those days, and therapy's come a long way since then. If you want my input, I'd suggest ignoring his letters when he's raging. Any reasons you give him, any admonitions, fall on deaf ears and merely give him fodder for arguing back. He's shown zero interest in listening to anyone who has a different point of view." *Look in the mirror, Mom.*

"So let me fill you in on Helen," I said, changing the subject before I risked blurting out something I'd regret. These conversations were too circular and familiar. "Now that Bruce is back, she's so much happier. Of course, 'happier' is relative. She still fusses about everything; right now she fears she's going to lose all her money and she needs to know exactly where it's being spent. I've sent copies of bank statements to reassure her, but I'm guessing it's old stuff being triggered and the impact of being placed in a home makes her extra paranoid. She'll go from 'you're doing such a wonderful job' to 'you're stealing from me,' then back again to how great I am in a single conversation.

"Did I tell you she had Myron take her to the bank, convinced I was stealing her money? She actually got the banker to open a new account. The only way I found out was the regular account was suddenly overdrawn. I spent a couple of hours trying to square it away, and had to send the bank a copy of the Power of Attorney to keep her from being able to do it again."

"Why would she do that?" She sounded genuinely puzzled. "She knows you're handling her money."

"Because she can't remember details from day to day. Plus she hates losing a sense of control. I understand it; I just can't let her mess up the banking like that. We've left her on one account so she still has a debit card for when she goes out. There's a chance she could lose it, but it's worth it for her to have some freedom. Same with letting her walk through the neighborhood. There's a risk she could be attacked or get lost, but restricting her movement feels wrong.

"She's losing so much I can't take everything away. And at this point she rarely goes out alone, since she doesn't want to leave Bruce. He gets annoyed with her constant fussing over him, but at the same time I can see how glad he is to be with her. I don't know what'll happen when he dies." I shuddered at the thought of going through a repeat of the previous fall.

"But how is her health?" my mom asked. "I've always said her body will go on forever. How is she holding up?"

"Strong as ever. It's her brain that's deteriorating; no signs of anything else. She doesn't even get colds that go through the place. We're managing her anxiety better with the meds she's taking, and it definitely helps that Bruce is with her. She's making a few friends and they spend time out of their apartment more. It's been good for her mental health."

"Yeah, well, my brain is fine; it's my body that's falling apart. She'll outlive me; I've always believed that." *Here we go again.* Another quick subject change was needed before she spun off into her jealousy of Helen.

"We'll see. In other news, Alan is thinking about quitting his job to go back to school. We've been planning it for a while and we're getting closer to pulling the trigger. He's been wanting to start his own business for years." I didn't reveal how close we actually were to taking action.

"What! What will you do for money? How will you be able to help m…" she cut herself off before she could finish the sentence. It didn't matter; I knew where it was going. I ignored it.

"We've been saving up for this and I'll keep working so we won't starve. He's interested in forensics, working in the legal field to help attorneys look at evidence that might be on someone's phone or computer. It's a fairly new area, and I think he'd be great at it with all his background in programming and testing," I went on.

211

"He's been researching it for quite awhile and has a friend who is already working in the field." As I filled her in on more details of our plans, I wondered if my mother would ever be concerned about my welfare other than how it impacted her. To be fair, she had been very helpful, flying in from New Mexico, where she was living at the time, to stay with me for the first three weeks after David's birth. She played with Janie, cooked and cleaned, ran errands, and in general kept things going smoothly as Mike and I adjusted to life with two kids. Those positive moments kept luring me into hoping she would somehow come through again, but those memories always seemed to be overshadowed by the times she failed so blatantly. My mother's first thoughts were all too frequently about her, and as time passed it seemed to be harder for her to hide it. Or perhaps I was just catching on faster.

Chapter 34

To: MontgJD@Montgomerylaw.usa
From: Gary.Wylings@qusmail.japan

Dear Mr. Montgomery,

I am writing you since Shelly has blocked all my attempts to have a civil conversation regarding the Allaway Trust. She has cut off direct contact and the only conclusion I can draw is that she is hiding something. It is my belief she must be colluding with the financial planners to somehow defraud me.

My mother is equally uncooperative and is protecting Shelly, something she has always done at my expense. She must be benefitting in some way from Shelly's actions. I want an accounting of every dime spent.

As the oldest male heir I demand certain respect and consideration, none of which I have received. I want to be included in every decision regarding the Trust, and expect to be named Co-Trustee. I hold Shelly responsible for any losses incurred while she is managing the money. I want the financial planners fired.

Gary

To: ShellyJ.123@qusmail.usa
From: MontgJD@Montgomerylaw.usa

Dear Shelly,

I received the above email correspondence from your brother. Since it's routine to have the work you are doing reviewed regularly I have no concerns about fraud. How would you like to respond to this? I can write him back and correct some of his misperceptions, and perhaps that will mollify him. Let me know.

Regards,

James

"Just when we thought it couldn't get worse, Gary comes up with more crap," I lamented to Alan after reading him the email over the phone. "Seriously, the 'oldest male heir' line again? What century is he living in? I know he's been hounding my mother with this garbage, but I didn't think he'd go to the attorney with it."

"Send me a copy of the email so I can look at it more closely. We don't need to do anything urgently, and we may not even want to respond at all. Give me a chance to sit with it, and it's probably good for you to sit with it as well." Once again, Alan was the voice of reason.

"I'm not sure where he gets off on this fraud crap. Why would I hide anything? It all has to be overseen by the attorney anyway when I do an annual report." I was still surprised that he'd gone down that road.

"He's looking for anything to get control. He figures if he can dig up any dirt to disqualify you, or at least what in his mind is dirt, he'll get his wish. I wouldn't worry about it. James was very clear it's irrelevant and nothing to stress about."

"I know, I know; it's one more load of bull to have to deal with. I'd hoped we could have calm for a while longer. Delusional me I suppose. Papa Paul would be rolling over in his grave if he heard this nonsense. I wish he were still alive to see it." I paused before continuing. "Okay, let's talk tonight and come up with our next strategy."

I hung up the phone and sat at the table, sipping tea and staring out the window. *Where does he come up with this stuff? And why?* My mind wandered all over the place, tracing threads that led back to childhood, my mother and grandparents, incidents over time, and my training as a therapist. My tendency was to understand the other person's point of view, to get a sense of what drove someone to act the way he or she did. I'd put myself in their shoes and find ways to feel compassionate toward their experiences even if I couldn't condone their actions.

But is this strategy helpful here? I've always seen Gary as the outcast, the one marginalized by everyone, the one who'd gotten into drugs, the one who'd struggled to find his way, but who had eventually managed to turn his life into something productive.

I pushed my chair from the table, grabbed my cup and walked into the kitchen. I filled the electric kettle with fresh water, and as it heated I pulled a tea bag from the box and tore it open. Adding milk and sweetener to the mug I leaned against the counter, my mind still puzzling over my brother.

The hissing of the kettle snapped me back to the present. Pouring the water into the cup, I stirred it slowly, watching the liquids blend into a milky blur. Thinking was helping me sort out my feelings. Alan had been right in asking me to wait before responding. It was forcing me to confront my own assumptions, just as I wanted Gary to do.

But I doubt he will. Dammit, I'm still doing it! I'm jumping to conclusions based on my experiences, and of course he's doing the same. But mine are right and his are wrong!

Even I had to laugh at that one.

My brain was spinning and I needed to make it stop. Picking up the phone, I called my friend Tori. We'd been partners in private practice before I moved from California to Washington, and we'd maintained our close relationship despite the miles separating us. Not only did Tori give me a different perspective with her years of experience as a therapist, she gave me privacy. I didn't want my current officemates to be involved in my personal life. They were supportive regarding clients and extremely helpful for case consultations, but we'd never extended those friendships outside the office, and that suited me just fine.

"Hey, got time to chat?" I asked when she answered the phone. "I need your listening skills and some advice if you've got a minute."

"I'm actually free," she replied. "My next client isn't for another hour and I was just sitting here avoiding paperwork, so good timing. What's up?"

I filled her in on the latest with Gary. We'd spoken a few times since Helen's crisis and subsequent move so she was familiar with the situation and the key players. But when we'd last spoken things were calming down.

"Here's the thing: I get so caught up in understanding his position and how crappy he had it growing up, and feel guilty getting mad at him as a result. I keep wanting to explain things to him, to find a way to include him without letting him take over, but every time I do it seems like we go farther down the rat hole," I concluded. "Help me figure this out!"

We sat in silence for a minute as Tori gathered her thoughts before speaking. "So your perspective is he's being unreasonable and won't listen to any other point of view. You want to keep trying to reason with him to get him to understand your actions and motives," she paused. "You want him to hear you out and then agree with you? Is that right?"

I thought for a moment. I didn't like the way that sounded and wanted to jump in with a good defense, but I'd known Tori long enough to trust that the question, if I let it percolate, would yield important knowledge.

"I see where you're going with this; we're each trying to persuade the other of the correctness of our positions, and neither appears willing to listen to the other. Is that what you're thinking? That I am being the same as he is? It's what I'd been spinning about when I decided to call you."

"I hate to say it, but there is some truth to that," Tori commented. "What's showing up for you?"

Damn therapist answer. "Part of it feels accurate," I acknowledged. Even if I knew the techniques Tori was using, they were still helpful. "I have to agree that on a deeper level if he would just see things my way we'd get along fine. It's his unwillingness, or inability, to do so that is making my life miserable. So I'll have to own that one," I admitted.

"I think there's more. I know he feels marginalized, and I know he still blames my mother for everything wrong that's ever happened to him, and wants me to concur. But jeez, I haven't lived with her since I was eighteen. Seems ridiculous to keep holding her accountable for my choices in life today. Even I can acknowledge that I don't believe my mother woke up every morning thinking, 'how can I screw up my kid today,' but instead, attempted to do her best although she failed with regularity. But he never married or had kids. I tried explaining this to Gary when he went off on a tirade against her years ago, hoping my perspective as a parent would have some impact on him, and shift his point of view to one more aligned with what I felt. Damn, I've been doing this a long time: hoping my explanations will change someone else."

I paused to sip my tea before continuing. "I keep thinking that if I can reassure him that he matters, he'll calm down and be reasonable. But at the same time, while I'd love to talk to him, hear his pain, and find ways to include him, I honestly don't believe he's interested in that, and no amount of empathy will turn this around. The only way forward for him is for me to concede on his terms, and I won't do that," I concluded.

"He's stuck in resentment, is that how it feels to you? That unless you somehow make up for all the wrongs done to him he'll never let go?" Tori inquired.

"Exactly. I've tried to hear him out; I've done that for years, but it keeps cycling through the same narrative over and over. The 'gee, it sucks' doesn't help, nor does the 'why don't you work on letting it go,' line. He's looking for something that I doubt he'll ever find as long as he's holding onto his resentment for mistreatments years ago. What a miserable way to experience the world!" I shuddered. "On top of that, he's incredibly belligerent and nasty."

"Is this behavior new?" she inquired.

"I think so, or at least it's newly directed at me. Maybe it's always been there and what my grandparents reacted to when they occasionally came to blows. But it does cause me to question what's going on in his head and reinforces why I think it's a waste of time to try to reason with him."

"So coming back to where we started," Tori responded, "it sounds a lot like you're aware you can get preachy and have to watch for that, but that Gary also gives you good reason for keeping your distance and disengaging from any conversations. So yes, you are most likely 'in the right,' but no need to gloat!" I heard the laughter in Tori's voice. "You can't ignore him because of your obligations to the Trust, but you don't have to try and work on improving the relationship either. Holding your boundaries while keeping your duties as Trustee clean toward him seems like the obvious course. Have fun with that, hahaha."

"Glad to see you're taking my side. But also nice to know you'd call me out if I were missing something. I appreciate that about you…or at least I appreciate it in theory!" I chuckled. "I may need to call you for reinforcement now and then. Gary still has a way of getting under my skin. I hope I can get past reacting; it's a waste of energy and I'm sick of talking about him," I admitted. "So, let's talk about something more pleasant. How are your kids?"

The conversation moved in a new direction, and after lots of laughter and catching up we finished the call. I felt relieved to have unburdened myself on someone besides Alan.

Chapter 35

"When I quit I want to take some time off to rest and regroup before starting school," Alan said one evening over dinner. "I'd love to take a vacation and unwind from these past few years. Helen's doing fine, and we can always fly home to see her if something comes up. We've definitely got enough in savings to see us through at this point."

"You know, in the past I would have argued with you to work till the last minute, but I actually agree with you. We need a break: from work, Helen, family, all the crap. How about taking the bikes and camping for a month?" I surprised myself with how readily I agreed. My comfort with Alan's decision to quit the company had been growing. Realizing how much my fears about health insurance and steady income had been driving my actions was an eye-opener. I'd never seen myself as that insecure; in fact I'd long held a self-image of one to rebound no matter the circumstances. But apparently what I'd been telling myself was partially fiction. It was time to change that story to reflect my newfound awareness, and Alan was thrilled.

"Let's set a hard exit date and get moving on it. If we want to go on the motorcycles, then maybe the first of September would be a good time? The weather should still be good enough for riding and camping, and if we go as soon as kids go back to school it won't be as busy with tourists. That gives us a few months to get everything ready. Your classes don't start till October anyway." I was somewhat shocked to feel no negative reaction to the conversation. I thought for sure my stomach would at least do a small summersault, but instead all I felt was excitement.

"I always thought I had to have it all together, to plan years in advance and know how I might deal with anything that came up. Ironically it was my mother who crammed that down my throat: 'always think of the consequences before you do anything,' as if she ever did that. I honestly believe she was training me to take care of her from the moment I was born.

"Funny how Gary and my mom still hold onto their anger at a parent for their predicaments, yet each hold contempt for the other for that exact reason. Amazing how little insight either of them has into their own behaviors. No wonder I decided to become a therapist: the joke in grad school was that most of us were there to fix our own families. In my case maybe it wasn't too far off the mark!"

"Well, thankfully you aren't your mother," Alan reassured me. "I wouldn't have been attracted to that aspect of your personality had it been there. I like your balance of risk and responsibility; it helps keep me grounded."

"True, we do complement each other. Your willingness to leap, and your belief you'll land just fine, forces me to want to do the same. But sometimes I still have to fight the urge to counterbalance you by holding on to things more tightly. This is a good exercise for me. I only wish the stakes weren't quite so high, but maybe that's the point. It wouldn't mean as much if it didn't matter as much."

I sat thinking for a few minutes before continuing. "I'm getting excited to see where this takes us. I like what it's doing for us, and I really like not having to do it all alone, that we're sharing this journey together. Again the irony: the more I let you see my vulnerabilities, the closer I feel to you. You'd think I'd already know that as a therapist, but it's one thing to read it in books, another to actually live it."

"I like your vulnerabilities," Alan responded, innuendo in his voice. "I'd like to see them for myself later tonight, as a matter of fact."

"Oh, I'll show you some vulnerability. Help me clear the table and load the dishwasher first; I find kitchen chores to be quite sexy in a man. Great foreplay if you ask me," I laughed. I was starting to get excited about more than our upcoming trip.

Chapter 36

"Hi, Shelly, it's Sharon. I wanted you to know that Bruce is in the hospital and it looks like he won't be coming out. He's got pneumonia, and Helen's refusing to leave his side. She's driving the staff crazy, but there's no reasoning with her."

I'd taken Kim's advice and hired a care manager. She had strongly suggested that since Helen wanted to stay in the Bay Area it was imperative to have someone close by for emergencies while her caregivers at Duncan House became her new family. With Helen still not completely settled, I'd already seen signs that Kim had been correct in her assessment.

The agency I'd selected hired retired nurses as care managers, and Sharon was a perfect fit for Helen. Their shared background made it easy for Helen to relate, and over the months they had formed a close relationship. Sharon visited weekly, which not only supported Helen, but also ensured the staff at Duncan House knew she hadn't been abandoned. She took her to medical appointments, out to lunch, and drives through her old haunts. While Myron managed his father's health needs, Sharon always included Bruce in their outings.

"I'm amazed he's lasted this long. Hard to believe he just

celebrated his one hundred and first birthday. Quite a life he's lived! And it sounds like Helen is doing exactly what she did with my grandfather: believing only she can take care of him properly. Any prognosis of how long he has? Obviously I'll come down to be with Helen." I'd talk to Alan later to see if he'd be able to join me. He didn't always go on my regular monthly visits, but it was definitely nicer when we were there together.

"Not long. Other than palliative care, they aren't going to treat him. The skin on his face is too frail for any additional surgeries and the cancer is spreading. He's been at peace with things since he came back to Helen, though privately he expressed his concerns about how she'll do without him here."

"Of course I'll go with you," Alan replied when I called. "It's got to be hard for her going through another separation from him, only this one is permanent. I'm glad at least they had some time together again." Alan had grown quite attached to Helen, having spent some of her worst moments with her.

"Okay, I'll make the arrangements to get a flight as soon as possible. Hopefully your work won't implode while we're gone."

"It won't. I've kept them fooled thinking I'm actually producing something. They have no idea I'm almost out the door; I've been so upbeat around here lately," he chuckled. It felt good knowing he was about to leave them in the lurch after all the time he'd been jerked around. He didn't relish the idea of letting down some of his workmates, but he didn't give a damn about his manager or the company.

Bruce passed quietly this morning. Helen was with him and was able to say goodbye. The nurses were great, letting her stay as long as she needed. Even Myron was agreeable, giving her space to grieve. I've taken her back to the apartment and told her you were coming. Consuela was with her when I left. I listened to the voicemail on the shuttle from the airport to the rental car lot. No need to call back.

We arrived at the now familiar facility and headed up to Helen's unit. I tapped lightly on her door, not wanting to startle her if she was upset. I heard footsteps approaching and her 'Who's there?' before the door opened slightly. Helen's head peeked out and her face perked up when she saw us.

"Shelly, Alan, it's wonderful to see you!" We exchanged hugs and stepped inside, putting our things on the side table in the entry. "Come sit down with me," she invited. We took up spots on either side of her.

"Helen, we're so sorry about Bruce," I turned to look at her. "We wish we could have been here to say goodbye. How are you doing?"

"I'm sad, but I'm doing fine," she smiled up at me. "I was with him when he passed. It was his time and he went peacefully. Did you know he had just celebrated his one hundred and first birthday?" She squeezed my hand. She reached for an envelope on the coffee table. "Here're pictures of the party we had for him in the common room downstairs. People were very kind and the kitchen even made him a cake. He enjoyed all the fuss, although he pretended he didn't."

I opened the packet and flipped through the photos. Despite his age and the facial damage, Bruce looked remarkably alert. Several of the pictures were of him with Helen, and I was glad someone had captured their last happy memories. By now I knew better than to ask about any of the other people at their small gathering. Over the last few visits I'd seen Helen struggle when we'd meet someone in the dining room or hallway, recognizing faces but not remembering names. The blessing of being at Duncan House, however, was that none of the other residents cared since many of them had similar issues.

"I'm happy you had him here with you as long as you did," Alan interjected. "He told me several times how much he missed you when he was gone. He really did love you, Helen." I could see her eyes misting in response to Alan's words.

"I know you loved him as well," he continued. "What a gift for you two to have found each other and been able to spend eleven years together. You were both so lucky."

"Yes, I was; we were. Although I never felt for him what I did for your grandfather," she looked at me. "It was a different kind of love but I would never have made it alone all these years without him. I was meant to be with someone. I like taking care of a man, and Bruce liked that."

"How did you meet Bruce?" Alan inquired. "I know it was before I met Shelly, but I don't think you ever told me the story."

"I was so depressed after Paul died, I really didn't want to live," Helen stated. "Shelly invited me up for Christmas that first year and I forced myself to go even though I just wanted to stay home and hide in my room.

"We went up to their mountain cabin, and it started to snow. And it kept snowing; so much we actually got snowed in! Janie and David took me out on the snowmobile, my first time ever on one. We cut a tree down from behind the house and decorated it for the holiday, very old fashioned with popcorn and paper chains we strung together. Christmas morning we awoke to a glorious day, the sun shining brightly and the air crisp and cold. It was magical for all of us." I still marveled at Helen's recall of events long past; it was such a contrast to her inability to remember something that had happened only minutes before.

"After that trip I felt something had changed. I began going out more, and started attending a support group for widows and widowers at San Toro General Hospital. Someone had suggested it earlier, but I wasn't ready. We met every other week, and after I'd been there maybe a month or two, this handsome gentleman came to one of our meetings. He was quiet and gentle, a retired welder but also a musician and sailor. His wife had died two years before." She stopped, as if picturing the moment he entered the room.

"How did you end up getting together? Is the widows' group the hot place to meet nowadays?" Alan asked playfully.

"We started talking, and found out we shared some common friends. He asked me to join him for dinner after one of the meetings and I said yes," she replied, ignoring his teasing. "We discovered we both loved the symphony, and both wanted a companion to still be able to travel. He'd even been in Roosters, like Paul.

"But I had no idea he was so much older than I," Helen sounded shocked. "I assumed we were closer in age. It wasn't until several months later I realized he was ninety, and I was only seventy-four! I always did like older men. But more importantly, I think Bruce was like me, better married than single. Despite my escapades as a young woman, I'm someone who wants to be with a man, to take care of someone. I hate being alone."

"I get that. I definitely prefer being married to your granddaughter," Alan smiled at Helen. "I think she'd agree with that as well: we're better together." I nodded.

Helen and I'd had these conversations many times over the years. We discussed how women of my age were often no longer content to stay home, especially if they didn't have children. I'd been able to have the best of both worlds: maintaining a professional career that allowed me to work part time when the kids were young. I sometimes wondered how Helen was able to leave her nursing behind when she and Papa Paul moved to San Toro, but they filled their lives with friends, travel and volunteer work. She never complained of being bored, and in fact, was a whirlwind of activity when I'd visit. I'd often help her out in the kitchen and we'd talk. Our conversations became even deeper after Papa Paul's passing, although they were less frequent after Bruce came along. With Helen's constant need to be doing something, to attend to his needs and fuss over him, it made it hard to focus for long, and easier to chat about light subjects that didn't require much follow-up.

I always wondered what would have happened if Helen and Papa Paul had had children together. I surmised it would have changed their closeness, having to find space for another in their very tight world. Papa Paul loved being the center of attention, the patriarch of the family, and Helen easily acceded the limelight to him. She preferred being the force behind the scenes, the one who made sure he was well tended to and always loved. The more I learned about them the more I understood their intense attraction. For Helen, it was far more than physical; it was the safety of being loved despite the shame she felt from her childhood. For him, it was most likely the security of knowing she would never leave him, that she put him first in her life. After the pain of his first marriage and the dismal years stuck in his second, that knowledge gave him the comfort he needed to freely express his devotion to her.

But now Bruce was gone, as was Papa Paul, and I wondered how Helen would cope. So far, she was doing far better than either Alan or I expected.

"Let's go get something to eat. We're starving, and I bet you'd like to get away from here for a few hours. I'm sure we'll find something across the street at the mall." It was a good excuse to walk around, keeping Helen occupied. Without Bruce as a distraction, I wasn't sure what we'd talk about. Helen's short-term memory issues created challenges with most conversations, and if she fixated on something it was often hard to dislodge her. While I loved visiting her, it was still exhausting spending long periods of time together.

The next two days passed in a pleasant mix of taking Helen out on drives, walking to the local hair salon for a much needed cut, and sharing meals. Despite moments of incredible clarity, I noticed more gaps in Helen's long-term memory and struggled at times to find topics to discuss that didn't prove too challenging for her. Her room was filled with photos we'd chosen of loved ones. She still remembered faces, but more often she could no longer recall names. Prompting would elicit memories of events, but with fewer and fewer details. I'd learned to treat her constant repetitions as if I was hearing them for the first time, but it was becoming a bit more taxing with each visit. My natural conversational style was to ask questions, digging deeper to learn more about the subject or the person. That didn't work with someone dealing with Alzheimer's, and on this trip it left me deferring to Alan to find a safe topic. He seemed to have endless patience with her, and Helen clearly appreciated him for it.

Chapter 37

The emails from Gary continued unabated, but thankfully, being funneled through the attorney made it easier to pause before even contemplating a reply. Most contained variations of the same theme: it was my fault Helen was in Duncan House, my duty to assign him as Co-Trustee, and imperative that I repent and confess the fraud of stealing monies from the Trust.

"It'd be laughable if it weren't so sad," I told Grace over lunch. "I'm having a harder time seeing him through the same lens I always viewed him through. I find myself saying 'I don't care' when he rants about childhood issues or his reasons for his demands. The more he pushes to connect with me over some slight he experienced, the less I'm inclined to do so," I reflected. "It's exhausting continually going down that road; my youth ended long ago and I'm much happier living in the real world. Too bad he can't figure out a way to join me here."

"Yup. I know I've had to take a few steps back from some in my family who can't see me for who I am now, but luckily it's only in one area, my leaving the church."

"In my past I've been the mediator, always seeing both sides of an issue and trying to find a way that works for everyone," I said.

"There's a lot of positive in that, but I struggle with where it's been harmful, especially to me; I wait too long, have too much compassion for someone who doesn't reciprocate. I fail to see when it's one-sided and I'm the only one open to hearing a differing opinion. I assume everyone is like me and it takes a slap upside the head before I finally see it."

"The main difference between your situation and mine is there are so many other deep connections that go beyond the church. They've never attacked me or tried to guilt me into returning to the fold; we mostly just avoid the topic," Grace observed. "With that one exception, we're close. While they struggle with the changes they see in me and worry about my eternal life, they still love and value me. Their concern is genuine, and having been there myself, I understand it. I'm not going to ask them to change just as I don't want them to ask me to change. Thankfully, we share other values and a lot of laughter."

"So they aren't forcing you to conform to their beliefs; they just silently pray you'll soon see the light again, huh?" I chuckled. "But you're able to let them do that as long as they both keep it to themselves and include you in their lives, and in their kids' lives. They aren't badmouthing you or threatening you. In fact, they come visit you often enough, and if they really saw you as evil I doubt they'd do that."

"Exactly. We've found a way to stay connected despite that difference. Love triumphs over their fears, I suppose. Whereas with your brother it seems to be the opposite: his fears and his resentments overpower any love."

"Yet he professes to love me. And maybe in his world it's love, but in mine it's having the opposite effect. It's driven me to the point where any feelings I had for him are gone. I've experienced my own variation of the stages of grief: What the fuck? Let me explain, Are you fucking kidding me? I miss who I thought you were, and finally, I don't give a shit." I laughed before continuing. "I have no desire to talk to him, see him, or share anything with him. I'm committed to my duties regarding the Trust and to him as a future beneficiary. But when Helen and my mother die, our connection ends. He's pushed me up to the edge and finally over."

I glanced out the window. I pictured a ribbon that had once connected us slowly shredding and finally tearing apart. As I thought about the metaphor, I felt nothing, and it was the nothingness that made me sad.

Chapter 38

I walked around the house one last time before picking my small black satchel off the floor and heading into the garage. Our gear was carefully packed, tucked into the side cases on the bikes or strapped onto the seats behind us: tent, sleeping bags, cooking kit, and computers, along with extra clothes and jackets should the weather suddenly turn.

We were finally leaving; one month on the road. Alan had left work the previous Friday on good terms and with no regrets, and my clients were given names of other therapists in case of emergencies. Handing the keys to the house sitter, I backed my bike out of the garage and waited for Alan to do the same. After my conversation with Grace, and later Alan, I waited to see if my fears would return, but they never did. I took it as a sign we'd made the right choice. All I felt now was excitement.

We'd plotted out the first few days of the trip, and a few hard dates we needed to honor that included visits at specific family events, but otherwise we decided to play everything by ear. Our lives had been so consumed by the demands of others that the freedom of no agenda was liberating.

"Ready," Alan said through the intercom system installed in our helmets.

"Ready," I called back, our signal that it was now safe for him to take off, with me following behind. We'd developed our routines over the years and each time we went through our checklist I noticed my anticipation building. It always meant we were headed on an adventure, and this was no exception.

Our first planned stop was San Toro. Camping two nights on the way south, we arrived at Duncan House in time for lunch. Without a car to take Helen, we opted to eat with the other residents in the dining hall and then walk to the local park we'd visited on occasion.

It'd only been a month since our last trip, but the changes in Helen were noticeable. She still remembered my name without prompting, but for the first time I noticed that while she lit up upon seeing Alan, she no longer seemed to recall his.

"Alan's so happy to see you," I offered, hoping the naturalness of mentioning it would cover her hesitation.

"Yes, Alan, it's a pleasure to see you, too!" she replied, not missing a beat. Another strategy to file away for future use. "They're starting to serve lunch so we should go into the dining room. I'm sitting at a new table now, since Bruce and I sat together with another couple before he died."

I waited, wondering if she would become emotional at the mention of him.

"A new man moved in, a handsome gentleman, and all the women are vying for his attentions," she continued. "I think he likes me, actually," she smiled.

I was pleased she seemed to be doing quite well and surprised she remembered so much about Bruce as we chatted. I'd heard stories of having to constantly remind family members of those they'd lost as their memories faded. Perhaps we would have to at a later date, but for now we enjoyed listening to her gossip, even if it was repeated numerous times.

After our meal, we walked outside to show Helen the motorcycles. We demonstrated how we communicated and pointed out where we stored things. She told us she had never been on a bike but had loved the thrill of speed when she skied as a younger woman. Once again our talk was a mix of detailed memories and huge lapses, but it was obvious the holes in the Swiss cheese were getting bigger. Occasionally I changed my inflection when repeating myself, but it really didn't matter; when she fell in a gap she was oblivious to having heard the same things only minutes before.

"How's your mother doing?" Helen surprised me with the question; she rarely asked about anyone anymore.

"She's settled nicely in Warm Beach; she seems to really like it there. You may remember she always enjoyed playing bridge and she's in a group of women now who meet weekly. I'm happy to hear she's doing it again." I stayed on safe topics despite the urge to have Helen confirm my opinions about my mother. "We plan to see her later on this trip." I knew she wouldn't remember that detail but it was nice to have snippets of normal conversation.

We walked around the block, Helen in between Alan and me. We each held a hand as if strolling with a small child who might run out in to the street. Visits with Helen had elicited my maternal instincts, and those feelings had only increased over time. Rather than being annoyed by the attention, Helen relished it.

"I remember how much she talked about physical affection, both with Papa Paul and Bruce," I said later that evening when we'd settled into our room. I'd researched camping near San Toro, but decided it was easier to stay at the now familiar hotel we used while visiting Helen.

"I think it's one of the things she misses the most about Bruce. I noticed that while she talks about him, she speaks more about my grandfather now. But the staff also mentioned how often she comes up for hugs. They hold her for a few minutes and she's happier. She still gets anxious and annoying at times, but since her move to Assisted Living after Bruce died she's closer to the nursing station, the front lobby, and the library, and seems a lot more settled. Her room is smaller, but there's so much more going on."

"Did you hear her actually use the word 'content' today? I was shocked. I never thought I'd hear those words out of her again. She said she was feeling 'content' at Duncan House. Who'd have guessed that?"

"I did hear it. I was probably as surprised as you were," Alan agreed. "After all the phone calls, complaints, and agonizing we've listened to over the past months I was happy to hear her say it, even if she doesn't remember it tomorrow. At least somewhere inside she's finding peace. I just hope it continues."

"Ditto. I do find it's easier to see her as she mellows. It seems she's left only with memories of emotions. Maybe that's why she remembers us still; she feels our love. I know she'll eventually lose her memories of us, too, but it's nice to have her this long.

"Sometimes I feel the urge to tell her all the crap going on with my mom and my brother. I wish I didn't have to bear that alone, and I know she'd be furious. On the other hand, I'm glad she's spared the knowledge that they are counting the minutes until they can get their hands on her money." I could feel my anger rising. "I get so pissed off every time I think about them and what they're doing."

"Thus, why we should stop talking about it and go down for Happy Hour. As I recall they have popcorn and wine, the perfect combination." I welcomed Alan's interruption. I reflected on the time I'd gone to the Happy Hour before everything had fallen apart for Helen. Had it really been eleven months already? So much had changed, and most of it for the better. But it had exposed how deeply dysfunctional my family really was. I'd always known on some level, but the events of the past year had forced me to see them, and me, through a new light.

Chapter 39

"I forgot how much I love to camp." We were sitting beside a crackling fire, heating water for dinner nearby on a small cook stove. "I can't say I love the freeze dried food, but since it's all we can fit on the bikes I'm slowly developing an appreciation for it. Reminds me of all the years I spent backpacking before kids. What would taste like crap anywhere else suddenly becomes palatable in the woods."

"I think cardboard would be agreeable to you right now," Alan mused. "You're definitely far more mellow than I've seen you in ages. We should've done this years ago."

"What, quit your job? Really? I'm not sure I could've handled it before. I wish I could say I'd have been fine, but I honestly think it took the chaos of Helen's life coming apart to rattle me enough to face my fears. Your job was too comfortable, too stable for me to consider chucking it for the unknown; I wasn't ready. I know you always say you'd be happy anywhere as long as I'm there. I wonder how much growing up watching my mother be so irresponsible with money tainted my views."

Spending unstructured days riding back roads and stopping late in the afternoons in time to set up the tent was the perfect antidote to all that had transpired over the past months. I felt myself letting go of the tension that had permeated every aspect of my being, and by the end of the second week we were once again having the deeper conversations we'd cherished before our lives had been taken hostage by the problems of work, Alzheimer's, and family.

"After college a bunch of my friends wandered across Europe, with no plans and only a Eurail Pass. I was envious but focused on the need to get fulltime work. I never even gave it a moment's thought to join them. I'd already been living on my own and paying most of my bills, working my way through school. At that time being unemployed was my biggest fear, and it wasn't even an option to consider something as frivolous as traipsing around the world. Looking back I was such an idiot to not take advantage of the opportunities to go before I got tied down." I picked up a stick to stir the campfire. "Amazing what we do to limit ourselves. How about you? Do you ever regret your choices?"

"Would I have done things differently?" Alan stared at the fire for a minute, considering the question. "Maybe, but I was never one to plan that far ahead. I've always trusted I'll land on my feet, so I've never really worried about it. Would I have studied harder in college, not gone into the service when I flunked out? It's not what happened, so I don't dwell on it. It's an interesting conversation for you, but it's never been one I've thought much about. I'm happy where I ended up, and I've had some great adventures getting here. Clearly not all have been wonderful," he paused, "but they all taught me something and got me another step along the way."

When we were first together Alan's 'but it's not what happened' comment drove me nuts. I loved looking at hypotheticals and pondering roads not taken. I liked imagining what life might have been like had we met in our twenties instead of marrying others first, or if I had taken the year off after college to travel. It wasn't that I was unhappy with how things turned out; it was more an exercise in creating differing storylines. But over the years I've grown to appreciate his definitive response, especially when the alternatives were potentially catastrophic. It's easier to let go of worries when I can tell myself 'well, that's not what happened,' than when I get stuck visualizing a disaster we just avoided.

"I guess part of me has to agree with you. When I got divorced people said stuff like 'you must have been meant to be together to have your kids.' I'd look at them quizzically and respond, 'well, if I hadn't married Mike I would have married someone else and had other kids. I wouldn't have known Janie and David.' They always stared at me, but it's true. If I hadn't met you, I wouldn't have known that I hadn't met you. My life would simply have gone another direction. My mom would say it's karma or the planets aligned perfectly. Nice sounding, but it's just another way to divert responsibility onto some obscure source. Then it's not her fault if she never met the perfect mate or didn't become a successful actress."

"So what do you blame when things go wrong?" Alan inquired. "Obviously not the stars, but what, or who?"

"I've never thought of it that way," I paused to reflect before continuing.

"My first reactions are often anger, so who am I angry at? Initially it's the person who's thwarting me, but then it becomes 'what did I do wrong?' so I think I actually blame myself for not understanding enough, or not anticipating something far enough in advance. That line of thinking has driven my behavior as long as I can remember."

"Where do you think it comes from?" Alan surprised me with his desire to dig deeper; that was usually my role.

"When I was maybe thirteen my mom told me she had been

shocked when she found out she was pregnant with me. She was trying to leave her marriage, was working in the city and planning her exit. Plus, she already had Gary who was still a toddler. At the time she hoped she'd miscarry, but of course, she didn't. Her point in telling the story was to reassure me that she was glad I'd been born. As an adult I understand her dilemma, but it was stupid to share it then because but all I heard was I wasn't wanted. But that's her, never thinking about what I might be feeling." I stared at the fire before continuing.

"Afterwards I had a dream about the conversation. In it, I believed she told me that story as a way to make me feel obligated to her. That I had wrecked her life by coming along at an inopportune time, making it harder for her as a single parent, with two kids instead of only one. I interpreted it to mean I owed it to her to care of her needs, to repay her for that burden."

"That's pretty crappy. But it's also an interpretation you made at a very young age, and in a vulnerable moment," Alan said.

"Yup. And it took me years to figure that out. Even now when I know it's ridiculous it can still grab hold of me emotionally. I feel pangs of guilt, and get caught in that urge to fix things, to own stuff that isn't mine."

"I can see that sometimes," Alan agreed. "But when I've pointed it out to you, instead of getting defensive, you listen. In my first marriage we wouldn't have known how to talk about it, and probably would have argued with each other or gone the silent route, burying it. Thankfully, it's different with you."

"I think we each learned a lot from earlier mistakes. But it goes both ways: when I tell you something that's important to me, you really listen. Even more, I see you incorporating it into your behavior. It reassures me that I matter to you," I said.

"Maybe that's my frustration now with my mother and brother: no matter what I say they don't seem to give a shit. I never noticed that with my brother before; I guess that's because I didn't expect anything from him. But it's reasonable to want a parent to care, and I've never felt heard by my mom. I got lip service, but her actions never changed; she did what she was going to do no matter what I said."

The fire slowly died down as we lapsed into a comfortable silence. I thought back on all the times my mother had lamented the distance between us, always trying to find a reason for it. I occasionally wondered what would happen if I did let down my defenses, but quickly dismissed the idea. It had never felt safe. Something always held me back.

After several more minutes of quiet, Alan suggested we turn in for the night. Pouring the water that remained in the cooking pot over the dying embers, he stirred the soupy mess until the fire was out. As I climbed into the tent, I realized that unlike many times, this evening's conversation wouldn't keep me awake. I felt settled and at peace.

Chapter 40

"Hi Mom!" I yelled through the closed door, dogs barking furiously in the background. "We're here!"

We arrived at the small cottage Ann shared with Julia and the menagerie of strays they'd accumulated. I always had a mixed reaction to visiting my mother: I looked forward to seeing her, but a larger part of me dreaded it. I knew how easily she could ask a question that put me on the spot and made me offer some kind of explanation that she would then dispute. The frustration that inevitably followed left me angry and drained. But driving past when so close wasn't an option; it felt wrong. So Alan and I strategized safe topics to discuss and how to disengage if Ann tried to lead me into dangerous territory. Best to keep it on neutral subjects and have him step in if it got out of hand, hopefully riding away with only positive memories.

I heard her yelling at the dogs to stop making so much noise as she pulled open the front door. "Shelly honey! So good to see you! And you, too, Alan!" Her greeting was warm and genuine, and I felt momentarily guilty for wanting to keep my distance.

"The dogs won't hurt you, they'll probably lick you to death," she went on, inviting us inside. "I've made lunch for you and it's ready, so let's sit and catch up," she pointed to the round table in the corner of the living space. "But before you do, did you see this couch I found and had recovered? It goes so well with everything else I had to have it." I glanced at the green leather sofa, the color blending nicely with the wallpaper behind it.

The room was filled with many familiar items from my mother's previous homes: knick-knacks and pictures, each with a story of some significance to her but none held any meaning for me. As always, I wondered at our vastly differing tastes, but perhaps that wasn't unusual for parents and children. After all, Janie's choices weren't the same as mine. But what struck me more than color schemes was overall style. My mother had to have a designer look, no matter the home, one of the many excuses she had for needing money. I felt a surge of annoyance and turned toward the table.

"It's very nice, Mom. What's for lunch? We're starved!" I moved to safe conversation.

"Tell me about your travels," she invited. "I still can't get over you riding a motorcycle! I'd be terrified. How did you ever get interested in it?" Her last question was directed to Alan, who easily filled the time with stories of needing cheap transportation during his Navy days and discovering a passion for two wheels in the process.

"Where's Julia?" I wondered where her roommate was. She rarely joined us when we visited, but normally made a quick appearance to say hello.

"She's at the track. It isn't racing season, but she enjoys off-track betting," Ann responded. "She likes it the way I like Bingo."

I bit my tongue, holding back irritation at the casual way she mentioned gambling as simply a form of entertainment when she refused to see how it impacted her finances. That, along with her three dogs and four cats would consume a large portion of anyone's budget, but the connection was lost on my mother. 'We have to have some pleasure' was always her reply. I'd once tried to help her understand that Alan and I made sacrifices when things were tight, but it never made a dent in Ann's thinking.

"Well, tell her we said hi," I said, keeping my voice neutral.

The conversation stayed on safe topics. Any time it threatened to detour Alan nonchalantly asked a question or re-directed it. I could see it was beginning to irritate Ann, who kept trying to bring it back to her usual topic of why her life was so challenging. At the two-hour mark I sensed we'd hit our limit and signaled to Alan it was time to leave. I felt a twinge of guilt about not wanting to stay longer, but I knew from experience things would deteriorate if we lingered.

Ann walked with us out to the bikes, asking questions about our set-up and our next destination as we put on our gear and readied to leave.

"I wish you could stay longer," she said. "I know you're always so busy, but I never get to see you or spend time with you."

"I know, Mom, it's hard to live so far apart. When you were in Seattle it was easier to meet for lunch or coffee. You moved too far away!" I wanted to keep things light. "Julia wanted a race track, and this was the best one for you guys." I made sure to keep the judgment out of my voice. "Besides, you said it's much cheaper here and the people are friendlier. I think it's been a good place for you two."

"It has been, it's just such a schlep for you to get here," Ann replied as we hugged goodbye. "Come visit again, and not such a short one next time!"

She stood by the driveway, waving as we put the bikes in gear and pulled out onto the road. I turned and waved one last time, feeling a poignancy that always hit when we parted. I wanted my relationship with my mother to be different, and I'd tried over the years, but it had never moved any closer. A mixture of emotions washed over me as we rode away: guilt, loss, and detachment. I wondered if it would ever change.

Chapter 41

Stops to visit Alan's family were intermixed with days of camping alone. Hours spent with his father and siblings were filled with laughter and telling stories, and it was hard to say goodbye when the time came to move on. I often imagined us living closer, spending holidays and birthdays together, enjoying each other's company. Alan had long ago made his peace with being the one who moved away, but their bonds, formed growing up on the farm in a house filled with love, were strong despite the miles. Each time we left we started planning our next visit.

"Why is it so different when we see your family versus seeing my mom?" I posed the question while we were stopped for a picnic lunch. "Why is it I can't wait to leave her but hate being so far from your brother and sisters?"

"They don't ask anything of us but to show up," he said thoughtfully. "They're busy with their own lives, but are generous with their time and attention when we come. Plus Tom loves to pick on me every chance he can. You'd think we were still kids on the farm!" he laughed.

"You may have hit on something. I've been trying to figure out what makes it so hard to feel compassion for my mother. I get it that she's older now, and can't earn much money. She probably does need some assistance, even if it's because of her poor choices. All she wants is to be closer and all I want is to move farther away. Your family is giving; my mother is selfish." The word came out unbidden.

"Bingo. You've bought into her reasons for years, why her life has been such a struggle and why she needs help, but I think you're finally peeling away the excuses. Bottom line: it doesn't matter how she got the way she is; she just is that way. Her needs come first," Alan commented. For once I didn't feel defensive.

"I just flashed on a memory from when I was a kid. My mom called me a 'selfish, egotistical brat' whenever she was mad at me. She'd scream and I'd cower, not understanding what the words even meant. In one of my attempts as an adult to get closer to her, I shared that memory with her. 'I never said that,' was her repeated response. I was dumbfounded, because the words were so vivid to me. Had I made it up? And if so, why? But I knew I hadn't. I'd heard it numerous times over the years, and had internalized the message, believing I had done something wrong and terrible.

"But you're right: her needs have always come first. She's good at pretending otherwise, but it keeps showing up despite her attempts to hide it. I guess it's why I need to keep up such a strong boundary between us. I've always had this vague sense that if I let her in she'd take everything, that nothing I gave would be enough." I tore off a chunk of baguette, reflecting on what I had just said. "All these years I've avoided labeling my mom as selfish. It's a harsh word, perhaps more so because it was used against me in such a hostile way. Geez, I was just a little kid and dependent upon my mom to protect me. The reality is it's my mom who's the selfish, egotistical brat.

"But then I wonder what it would be like if she woke up one morning and realized, 'Crap, I've been wrong all along; I wasn't the victim, I've made unreasonable demands on everyone, and my life really was the product of the choices I've made.' How does one live with that knowledge? What if she suddenly believed her entire life was a mistake and she's to blame for where she's ended up instead of it being the fault of the universe, or her father, or whatever?"

"It might make it easier for you to be closer to her, but realistically it ain't gonna happen. She's had far too many opportunities to see it differently and hasn't," Alan interjected.

"True. On top of that my mom has Julia, who reinforces her story of victimhood. Whether that's a good thing or bad I don't know. I bet my mom feels closer to Julia than me, and in a weird way that's freeing. She has someone who supports and understands her, and at least as a friend, loves her. Maybe I can simply be happy for her." I paused to take a sip of my drink.

"I remember what Kim mentioned when I first met her," I said, putting my cup down on the table. "That the struggle with Helen would be to accept who she is now, not what I need her to be. While it's not for the same reason, ultimately I think I need to let it all go with my mom. Stop asking her to be something else in the same way I want her to stop wanting something different from me. She is who she is, and it's up to me to accept that, and I mean really accept it, not just give it lip service." I looked at Alan as if expecting an answer. He sat, letting me work out my own conclusion.

"But will that alter what I do? I don't think so, other than helping me feel more peaceful about her. Maybe it's unfair to ask her to give up her victimhood view at her age, but it's okay to say no when she pulls the guilt crap. But what about Gary; why is he such a pain in the ass?"

"Unlike your mom, his resentment is overt, and his rage is hurtful, not just guilt inducing," Alan suggested. "And on top of that no one seems to be agreeing with him. Not you, your mom, or your grandparents in the past. He has no partner, no kids. No one's on his side."

"You mean you think maybe he's trying to get me to include him in all the trust stuff so he isn't so isolated, and not just for control? If that's true then what an incredibly sad place to be," I sighed. "Wow, I even feel some shred of compassion when I think about it from that perspective. But no matter where it's coming from, he's still actively inflicting pain and I'm going to protect myself."

"I agree. It's one thing to have an opinion; it's another to impose it on others," Alan replied. "If your mom simply blamed karma I doubt we'd be having this conversation. It's that she's expected you, Papa Paul, Helen, or for that matter anyone, to fix it for her. With Gary, he demands you do things exactly his way, there's no compromise, and he's furious when you don't. He won't let you make room for him. Obviously, we all hold views that we think are right, but we don't get to make those we supposedly care about do our bidding as a result."

"Fair enough. Of course, this discussion presumes they have even a modicum of self-awareness, and I've seen zero evidence of that. And it also assumes our views are the correct ones and theirs are wrong. Who knows, maybe we have it all backwards. Obviously, Papa Paul and Helen were on the same page as you and I, so as far as the Trust goes I won't budge. Doesn't matter if it's right, it's what they wanted. And neither Mom nor Gary gets to define who I am or how I behave; in that sense their behavior is irrelevant to me. I'll still make decisions as if we did have a good relationship, I just won't let them close to me emotionally." Summarizing my thoughts out loud was helpful.

"Your mom'll still try to push your buttons; you just don't have to judge her for it," Alan observed. "She is who she is, and has as much right to her views as you do to yours. You need to treat her with the same respect you want from her: let each other be.

"As for Gary; he gets to be as resentful as he wants without you attempting to change that. But unless he gives some indication he's open to listening to facts about the Trust, it's not worth trying to reason with him."

"As you've said many times before, and I guess you'll say many times again," I laughed. I rustled through our food bag and pulled out a couple of cookies, handing one to Alan.

"Shifting gears, I wonder how Helen will be when we see her? When I talked to Sharon earlier today she said Helen's memory is diminishing even more rapidly than before, and not just short term; she actually forgot her brother's name a few times, which is highly unusual. I hope she still remembers us."

"It doesn't matter if she does, it matters that we keep visiting," he responded. "It's as much for you, and me, as it is for her. You like seeing in person that she's okay, that she's doing well. You care about her."

"I do. I always have, but it's changed as she's declined. It's funny, but as her memory fades she's become even more approachable. She's less fussy, less busy. She's stopped worrying about making sure I'm okay and is more comfortable sitting. As her past recedes, she seems freer herself, less tied to the shame and pain she's held in all her life."

I paused to pull my thoughts together. "For much of this year I've been dwelling on the loss of her guidance and support as we've been dealing with everything. But maybe she's still teaching me. Yes, she's had a ton of trauma in her past, but I'm seeing love becoming her dominant emotion, especially as her stories are fading. You know, Alzheimer's may be the ultimate therapy tool to wash away not only the good stuff, but the crap as well. I'd never wish that on anyone, but since we didn't get a choice in the matter I can at least see some positive for her."

"No, I don't think anyone would want this awful disease, but you're right, she's been increasingly relaxed the last few visits. I don't look forward to where it might go from here, but at least it's okay for now," Alan agreed.

"So by letting go of any angst now, while I still have a choice, when my mind eventually goes, maybe I, too, will be left with only the feeling of love," I concluded. "Holding on to anything else seems like a waste of time."

Chapter 42

The final planned stop was where we started, visiting Helen. Alan and I were ready to get back to Seattle and the new prospects ahead of us, but the diversion to San Toro was welcomed as a chance to see Helen. The month off had provided the respite we'd both needed, giving us time alone and time to process all that had happened in the past year. After all the conversations with Alan I felt a sense of peace toward my mother and Gary; they weren't going to change and I no longer needed them to.

We checked into the same hotel, which now felt like our home away from home after so many visits, and carried our gear to our room on the fifth floor. Dumping our saddlebags on the bed, I stripped off my motorcycling garb and headed straight for the shower to clean up before donning street clothes. Duncan House was within walking distance and we planned to leave the bikes behind, strolling the few blocks to see Helen.

Over the year my feelings had shifted from anxious to see how she was doing to simply wanting to spend time with her. While Sharon kept me filled in on Helen's health and moods, I wanted to see her for myself. Even the pressure to fill the air with conversation was fading, and after the quiet of the trip I felt a greater comfort with silence.

I'd called the nurses' station to let them know when to expect us so they could help Helen get ready. From past experiences, I knew it was better to give her as little warning as possible to help manage her anxiety. Anything more than an hour of anticipation turned to fretting and bothering the staff, fearful she had missed our arrival when she couldn't keep track of the time.

She was waiting in the lobby when we arrived, neatly dressed in a mismatched outfit she'd never have been caught dead in before, but now was oblivious to. She lit up when we came through the door, dispelling any fears I had that she wouldn't remember us. Rushing up to greet us, she snuggled into my arms for a few moments before turning to Alan and his welcoming hug.

"Alan's so happy to see you!" I exclaimed, giving Helen his name before she had time to struggle to find it. "Would you like to go for a walk before it's time for dinner? Maybe to the park?"

October in San Toro was still quite pleasant, no need for sweaters or jackets, and we strolled casually the few blocks to the park. Helen delighted in our company, holding hands as we walked by various gardens and the small playground, filled with the laughter and chatter of young children climbing on the bars and careening down the wide metal slide. A father cheered as his son learned to ride his bicycle without training wheels for the first time, wobbling along the path and gaining confidence with each rotation of the pedals.

Helen stopped to watch, smiling as she took in all the sights and sounds. The three of us stood for a while, simply enjoying the activity before continuing down the path and heading for the small lake in the center of an open green space. We'd come to this park on previous visits, and I'd often felt pressured to find topics of conversation, as if to reassure Helen that she was getting my full attention during our short time together.

Alan directed us to a bench across the bike path from the lake, positioning Helen between us. Without speaking, I took one of her hands and held it gently. The sun warmed us from behind, casting glimmers of light on the gently swaying water. I watched as a flock of ducks glided smoothly in front of us.

"Look at that duck," Helen remarked, pointing to a large drake poking his head in and out of the water, searching for something to eat. "He's so big."

"He is," I commented. "He's certainly a big one."

We sat in silence for a few more moments.

"Did you see that big duck?" Helen asked. "He sure is busy."

"He certainly is," I replied. "He's looking for something to eat."

The honks and quacks of the waterfowl echoed around us before Helen spoke again.

"I like watching the ducks," she stated.

"Me, too," I agreed.

"Look at that big one there," Helen pointed. "He sure is busy."

"He certainly is," I said.

"Did you see that big one?" Helen asked.

"I did," I replied. "He sure is busy."

I glanced over Helen's head at Alan. He was leaned back, relaxed. His eyes were closed, and his face looked as peaceful as mine felt. It wasn't only Helen who had found contentment. Watching the ducks, there was no need for more; sharing the moment with two of the people I loved most was enough.

Gazing out across the water, I gently squeezed Helen's hand, sighing softly as a smile slowly spread across my face.

Acknowledgments

Thank you, as always, to Terry for your unwavering support, honest feedback, and gentleness. A shout-out to my family and friends who offered love, laugher, and a lot of wine as I navigated this journey. Hats off to my pre-readers who took the time to share your perspectives and critiques, giving me the push to make the story better, and to Jami for kindly letting me know when I've said enough. Pete, you captured it perfectly.

A deep debt of gratitude to the doctors, caregivers, and others along the path, helping me understand Alzheimer's and providing such compassionate care to all those who suffer from this disease.

And a special thank you to Amy, whose love never faded even as her memory declined. I still miss you.

Made in the USA
San Bernardino, CA
29 November 2017